BOOK
THREE
GUARDING HER HEART

Never Hire a Hero

REGINA SCOTT

*To those who love Regency romances, thank you for
reading my books all these years! And to the Lord, who
holds us through every Christmas.*

CHAPTER ONE

Near Alldene Castle, Surrey
Early December 1825

OF ALL THE enemies he'd faced over the years, he'd never thought two boys would be the most daunting.

Stephen Roth leaned back against the squabs of the coach that was trundling west toward Alldene Castle, the site of his new assignment. The winter landscape seemed as bleak as his thoughts. His fingers fisted in his lap.

"You are exactly what the countess needs," Lady Belfort said as she sat across from him.

She, at least, seemed to have no misgivings. Roth appreciated that about her. From the swan's down edging her quilted winter cloak to the embroidered wool skirts peeking out below, his patroness was the epitome of good taste and propriety. Her hair was as dark as his, her eyes a remarkable lavender. She must have been enamored by the color, for her gowns and coats inevitably matched it.

"I will endeavor to bring only praise to your efforts, your ladyship," he said.

She cocked her head. "Why, Mr. Roth, if I didn't know better, I might think you were nervous."

She didn't know the half of it. He had served his king and princes for most of his life, but they had elected to either return to their home country, Batavaria, or start new lives here in England. He could not return to Batavaria, and so far, his life in England had been less than what he'd hoped.

An Imperial Guard, a member of that elite force, renowned across the Continent for bravery, skill, and honor, reduced to guarding a steam manufactory at night.

And now, becoming a tutor.

A movement across the coach caught his eye. Fortune the cat arched her back and stretched before affixing him with her copper-colored gaze. Roth did not so much as smile, but he wiggled a finger against his trousers.

Fortune lowered her head, watching.

"You are teasing her," Lady Belfort said with a smile.

"I never tease." Roth wiggled his fingers again, and the cat leaped across the coach to pounce on him.

He raised both hands. "I surrender."

As if well pleased with herself, Fortune began rubbing against his thigh.

"We will need to watch her closely at the castle," Lady Belfort said. "I understand it has far too many places to hide should she escape." She nodded out the window. "You can see it now."

Hand running down the cat's grey fur, he glanced out the window. On a hill overlooking a narrow valley split by a winding stream, Alldene Castle glowed like gold in the light of the winter sun. A square tower guarded each of the front corners, with a wider gatehouse in the middle. A bailey with a crenelated top led from one to the other. It was shorter than the Great Keep of Batavaria, and stouter than the castle they had stayed in while in the German states. Still, he could appreciate the fortifications. If they had their own water supply, they could hold out against a siege for months.

Not that anyone would lay siege to them in Surrey. Worse luck.

The closer they came, however, the more he frowned.

Were those pitched rooftops right up against the bailey? A well-placed arrow could light the whole structure on fire. And the windows on the ground floor were far too wide to allow for protection.

But he had to own it was nice to hear the drawbridge rattle as the coach crossed it.

"They still have a moat," he said.

"I imagine you're one of the few to appreciate that fact," Lady Belfort replied as the carriage drew to a stop in the cobbled inner courtyard.

He had been right about the house. Shaped like a U, it filled the inside, from stone wall to stone wall. It was half timbered, the panels scrubbed white between thick, tarred oak beams, and the windows consisted of dozens of tiny panes of glass shaped like diamonds.

"Built in the sixteenth century," Lady Belfort commented. "But modernized since, I have heard."

That would account for the larger windows on the outside. Modernization was all well and good, so long as it kept the family safe.

A tall fellow with pomaded hair the same golden color as the castle walls and the regal bearing of a butler appeared from the doorway along the back of the courtyard as a footman jogged forward to open the door. Roth jumped down, then handed Lady Belfort to the grey stones, Fortune secured in her arms.

"Lady Belfort, Mr. Roth," the butler said with a bow. "Welcome to Alldene. Her ladyship is expecting you. If you'd be so kind." He waved toward the doorway.

The entire time, he smiled. As if having them there was such an honor he could not help but puff out his chest. Perhaps it was Lady Belfort who had impressed him.

Roth followed her and the butler into a dimly lit corridor that stretched in either direction, then accepted Fortune from her so another footman could take her cloak. The cat wiggled against his coat, but he kept his hold gentle. He wasn't entirely certain why Lady Belfort had brought her pet, but he would do nothing that might endanger Fortune. She was a legend, having matched a dozen well-placed lords over the years, including his own prince, Otto Leopold.

As he waited, he glanced around. After what he'd seen outside, he could only conclude that the occupants of Alldene Castle had trouble making up their minds about their home. The two-story entry hall just ahead was paneled at the bottom with dark wood, while a gallery of the same wood loomed over the left side. Along with the stone hearth and suit of armor in one corner, it should have been a brooding, masculine place. But every bit of the wood was elaborately carved in flowers, and the burning fire could only be called cheery.

As Roth handed Fortune back to his patroness, the butler turned left and led them down the corridor and around another corner. The southwest quadrant of the castle, then. The fellow opened a paneled door to let them into a long withdrawing room. Again, the walls were covered with the dark paneling, highly polished here, and it covered the hearth as well, but the expanse of carpet showed medallions of roses, and all the furniture was dainty and elegant and done in shades of pink or cream.

That elegance was nothing to the woman who stood as they entered. He'd seen Lady Alldene when he'd been helping his friend, Tanner, guard a railway opening last month. She was tall, willowy, and always draped in black, as she was now. The net veil flowed from her pale blond hair to the hem of her unornamented black gown.

"Lady Belfort, Mr. Roth," she said. "Thank you so much for coming."

Lady Belfort went to sit beside her on one of the velvet-upholstered sofas. Roth started toward the wall, to take up his usual spot, before realizing he didn't need to watch the room. He wasn't here to protect the countess, just her sons.

Even if something inside him urged him to protect her.

Habit. She might appear as if a good wind would bowl her over, but she likely needed no protection here in her great castle with her doting staff. Even now the butler was adding more coal to the fire as if to ensure her comfort.

Roth took a chair not too far away from the ladies and rested his hands on his knees.

Lady Belfort released Fortune, who slipped away from her to crawl into the countess's lap. Some of the tension in his shoulders eased. If Fortune approved of you, you were of very fine character indeed. He should not wonder that she appreciated the lovely countess.

He still remained astonished that she approved of him.

"I see you brought a friend," Lady Alldene said. Her long-fingered hand stroked the silky coat.

"I always take Fortune with me, so long as it is safe for her," Lady Belfort confessed. "She has a great gift for understanding people, far more than I will ever possess. She is very fond of Mr. Roth."

As if she knew her cue, Fortune jumped down onto the flowered carpet and padded toward him. She wound her way around his boots, purr audible against the pop of the fire.

"I will own to finding that comforting," Lady Alldene said with a look his direction.

He stopped himself from bending to pet the cat. Comforting? Did she have doubts about him?

What had she heard? Who would have told her about his past?

"Indeed," Lady Belfort said with a nod his direction. She turned her gaze on the countess once more. "You can understand why I am protective of my guards. I agreed to find them suitable positions here in England. Mr. Roth has not been appropriately appreciated so far."

He hadn't realized she'd noticed. He had done whatever work was given him without complaining.

"Well, we will do our best to appreciate his talents here," Lady Alldene said. "Felden, would you make sure Mr. Roth's things are taken up to the tutor's room?"

"Of course, your ladyship," her butler assured her.

Lady Belfort held up a hand as if to stop him. "First, I have a few questions of my own. I understand you are engaging him as a tutor for your two sons, Lord Shaw and Master James."

Lady Alldene inclined her head. "That is correct. I have a nurse for Audra, my daughter."

That was to the good. He was never sure what to do with little girls. They seemed so…breakable.

"And you wish him to school them in all the gentlemanly arts," Lady Belfort persisted.

"Reading, mathematics, geography, the sciences," Lady Alldene rattled off, each word a stone dropped into his stomach. Would she sack him immediately if she knew he had studied those things for only two years after joining the military?

"And of course riding, fencing, archery, and fisticuffs."

He blew out a breath. Those he could do. Those he excelled at.

"Very good," Lady Belfort said. "He will need a half day off each week, the opportunity to attend services on Sundays and holy days, and his own room as well as board."

"Certainly," the countess said. "And a mount at his disposal."

That could be a boon. He might take a ride once the weather was warmer, see something outside the castle walls.

Which oddly felt as if they were closing in.

"Then we are agreed," Lady Belfort said as if she'd finished negotiating the price for a new length of lace.

"Only one thing remains. I would like to have Fortune meet your children."

From the moment Thea had seen the cat, she could tell that Lady Belfort and Fortune shared a great bond. Still, she hadn't expected her new friend to bring the creature with her to Alldene, and she certainly hadn't expected her to want to introduce Fortune to the children.

It was going to be difficult enough introducing them to her sons' new tutor.

She couldn't help glancing at the fellow again. Did that chiseled face ever smile? She'd wanted someone sufficiently stern to cow her nemesis, Lord Westerbrook. But those steely grey eyes could likely give at least James, her youngest son, nightmares.

Perhaps she had made a mistake.

No! That fear had raised its head far too many times since Thomas had died. She was Lady Alldene, a countess in her own right. She had been born in this castle, she had grown up in this castle, and she had been trained to rule this castle and all the lands surrounding it. She didn't need anyone.

Most of the time.

"Felden," she said to her butler. "Would you be so kind as to ask Nurse Waters to bring the children down?"

"At once, your ladyship."

At least Felden seldom argued with her. He had been head footman when the butler she'd known growing up had retired and had been a logical choice to promote, Thomas had said. She'd agreed. Felden was organized, polished, and efficient, with a surprisingly affable nature for a butler. She could not ask for more.

But what should she ask of this man?

He was watching her now, eyes narrowing, as if he saw

the worry flickering inside her like a guttering candle. She raised her chin and met him look for look. She might wonder over tenant questions and tithes, but she was unwavering in one area.

The protection and happiness of her children. If this man could keep them here in the castle, she would be willing to give him anything.

Lady Belfort rose and went to collect her pet, who was still strolling back and forth around Mr. Roth's boots as if polishing them to ensure he would look tip-top for the coming introduction. She was a lovely creature, with silvery grey fur and white around her throat like a cravat. She gazed at Thea with eyes the color of copper kettles, tail swinging idly back and forth, as her mistress resumed her seat.

"I do hope you and your family will join us for our Christmas Eve party," Lady Belfort said. "We have held it every year since I was a girl. The pond generally ices up, so there should be skating. And if this weather holds, we might even have snow for sleigh rides and snowball fights."

The last word seemed to tug at his lips, for they twitched. Yes, she would imagine fights of any kind would amuse him.

"That sounds lovely," Thea said, focusing on her friend. "I'm sure the children would enjoy it."

As if in answer, her children's nurse trotted into the room, one hand holding Audra's. Nurse Waters was ample in appearance but a bit parsimonious in praise, though she had given Thea good service since coming here at Shaw's birth. Thea's ten-year-old son stood on one side, nose up and face smooth. Eight-year-old James, on the other side beyond Audra, was glancing around as if trying to determine what he might have done to be required so suddenly. Both favored her more than Thomas, though their hair was closer to brown than blond, their eyes a darker shade of blue.

"Children," Thea said, beckoning them closer. "You remember Lady Belfort from the railway demonstration last month. You may also remember Mr. Roth."

Dark-haired Audra brightened until she looked so much like her father that Thea's heart clenched. "You fought off those bad robbers."

"There are no good robbers, silly," Shaw pointed out with a shake of his head.

Audra's smile faded, and she glared at her brother.

"Mr. Roth was indeed a hero that day," Thea said. "That is why I suggested to Lady Belfort that we might hire him as your tutor, boys."

James' brows shot up. Shaw crossed his arms over his chest. But before he could start the rebellion she could see simmering in his eyes, Audra pulled out of the nurse's grip.

"Can't he be my tutor, too?" she begged. "I want a tutor, Mother."

"Girls don't have tutors," Shaw said. "They have governesses. And you're too little for one anyway."

She stomped her foot. "Am not!"

"Are so," Shaw countered.

"He's probably right," James hazarded.

"Children!" Thea rose, face hot. Thomas had always known what to say, what to do, to bring out the best in them. Was she such an unnatural mother that she couldn't do the same?

Lady Belfort opened her arms and allowed her pet to drop to the carpet.

Once more, Audra's face lit. "Kitty!"

Fortune shook herself as if shuddering.

"She isn't too fond of that word," Lady Belfort said with a smile. "Her name is Fortune, and she would like to make your acquaintance."

Waters took a step forward, round face pinching. "Your ladyship, I must protest. Cats are filthy things, better suited to barns and such."

Lady Belfort stiffened. "I can assure you, madam, that Fortune is bathed regularly and brushed twice daily. She is no more filthy than you are after a day of chasing children about."

Waters puffed herself up.

"Thank you, Waters," Thea said. "That will be all."

Her nurse swiveled and marched herself out.

In the meantime, Fortune had prowled closer to her daughter. Audra dropped to the carpet in a pool of muslin and held out a hand. "Nice cat. Lovely cat. Would you like to be friends?"

Shaw snorted. "Cats aren't friends."

"She *looks* friendly." James knelt beside his sister, who was petting the cat with such tenderness that Thea could only smile.

"If you don't need me, Mother," Shaw said, "I was in the middle of plotting strategy."

Her heir might pretend to great sophistication, but she knew the strategy he was devising had to do with the hundreds of lead soldiers who were endlessly battling across his bedchamber. At least he hadn't started to behave with the condescension of Lord Westerbrook. What he really needed was a father, but she wasn't ready to give him one. She might never be ready to give him one again.

Fortune had pulled away from Audra to suffer James' touch. A smile curved her youngest son's lips, one of the first she'd seen in a long time. Again, her heart twinged.

Then the cat approached Shaw.

Shaw looked down his nose at her.

Fortune sat, gazing up at him, head cocked, as if considering.

Thea thought she wasn't the only one holding her breath.

Fortune turned and went back to Audra and James.

Shaw sagged as if he knew he had somehow failed.

Thea glanced to Lady Belfort, who rose. "Two out of three isn't bad," her friend said. "I'm sure we can improve the odds in the future. I believe Mr. Roth can stay."

Shaw's head came back up. "So, we're to have Mr. Roth as our tutor, are we? I should think I would have a say in the matter."

The challenge was entirely too clear. Thomas would have known how to defuse the situation. She was highly tempted to send her son to his room until he apologized.

But she was interested in seeing how this man would take such a challenge.

She turned to Mr. Roth. "Well, sir? What do you think?"

CHAPTER TWO

H E HAD NEVER run from a challenge, and he didn't intend to start now. Roth rose to his full height and faced the lad across the impossibly flowered carpet.

"What do you require in a tutor, Lord Shaw?" he demanded.

The boy blinked, as if unused to anyone questioning him. Then he raised his chin. "Have you attended a prestigious college, sir?"

His mother shifted, as if she very much feared his answer.

"Yes," Roth replied. "I attended His Majesty's Academy for the Military Arts, where I learned all manner of history, strategy, and tactics."

Lord Shaw took a step forward, gaze lighting, then he shook himself. After all, a challenger shouldn't admit to any admiration for the enemy, at least in public. "And how many others have you tutored?"

"More than two dozen over the years." The boy didn't need to know they had been newly recruited members of the Imperial Guards, all Roth's age or older.

"That's very good," his brother said, looking to Lord Shaw as if for agreement.

Lord Shaw narrowed his eyes. "Have you ever been disciplined for an infraction?"

"Not in my career," Roth said, though his back twinged as if feeling the first lash of punishment even now. He didn't count his previous work in the Batavarian silver mines as a career. His life had changed when Captain Wyss, the former head of the Imperial Guard, had come recruiting. Even imprisoned criminals could help their king protect his people from Napoleon.

Lord Shaw glanced to his mother, brow furrowed. "I suppose he'll do."

He could almost feel the tension leaking out of the countess, like water escaping a thawing pond in spring. "I'm glad we are in agreement." She looked to Roth. Behind the veil, it was hard to see her eyes, but he thought he saw something sparkle in the depth of blue.

"Mr. Roth," she said in her clear, calm voice, "we'll leave you to settle in this afternoon. This evening, I'd like to hear your thoughts on the curriculum." She turned to Lady Belfort.

He knew a dismissal when he heard one. He had to stop himself from clapping his fist to his chest in salute. The butler stepped forward with a smile, as if to usher him to his new quarters.

Lord Shaw intercepted him. "Actually, Mother, I think it fitting that James and I show Mr. Roth around. A good soldier will want to know the lay of the land."

Had the boy studied the art of battle, then? Or had his father been a soldier as well? Roth didn't recall anyone mentioning Lord Alldene's history.

"I want to go too," the little girl proclaimed, rising from beside Fortune.

The cat came to wind around Roth's boots as if she very much wanted to join them. He bent, scooped her up, and presented her to Lady Belfort. The look Fortune cast him told him she was not amused by such treatment.

"Mr. Roth," the countess said, voice tighter, as if she was trying not to sigh, "will you allow it?"

The two boys, certainly, but the little girl? He had become acquainted with two near her age, daughters of

Sir Matthew and Lady Bateman. So much movement, so many questions. Yet Lady Audra was regarding him with every inch as much challenge as her older brother. Did the trait run in the family?

He inclined his head. "Lead the way, my lord."

Lord Shaw strolled from the room, his siblings scurrying in his wake. Roth brought up the rear.

The lad nodded to the left down the darkly paneled corridor. "That's the formal dining room at the end, there. You won't need to see it. I expect you'll be taking your meals with the staff."

"I expect as much as well," Roth said.

He frowned slightly, as if he thought Roth should have taken umbrage at the haughty tone, especially from someone who barely reached the middle of his chest.

"The other way is the chapel," he continued. "We have services there on holy days. Most Sundays we attend services in the village. We ride in the carriage. The servants walk behind."

Could that nose be any higher? "Good to know," Roth said.

Lady Audra had been bouncing up and down on her satin slippers. "And at the end," she put in, "is the armory. We have lots of swords and halberds and pikes."

Roth eyed her. "What is the difference between a halberd and a pike?"

Lord Shaw drew up short. "You don't know? I thought you were a soldier!"

Roth affixed him with a look that made him drop his gaze. "I know," he told the boy. "I want to hear that your sister knows."

Lady Audra nodded eagerly, setting her jet-colored curls to bouncing beside her face. "The two are both long and pointy, but the pikes have a little hook near the top and the halberds have an ax on them, so you can cut things in half." She sliced her arm down as if to prove as much.

Roth stuck out his lower lip. "Very good, Lady Audra."

She twisted from side to side, swishing her skirts. "Father told me."

"Yes, well, we needn't go into raptures about it," Lord Shaw said. He started down the corridor toward the front door. "I'm sure Mr. Roth would rather see the fortifications."

The footman on duty quickly opened the door for them, though he cast Roth a considering look. They came out into the inner courtyard. A winter breeze swept down from the crenelated walk, whipping up little eddies of dust, and Lady Audra shivered. He positioned himself closer and between her and the wind as her oldest brother stalked across the cobbles for the entry arch.

"Those still work," he said, tipping up his head to eye the pointed ends of the portcullis where it hung snugged up against the stone. "There are two of them, one at the front of the castle, and one here at the courtyard. And those," he went so far as to point up at square holes in the wooden ceiling between the two gates, "are murder holes."

"The guards used them to pour boiling oil down on our enemies," Master James said. "We still have the cauldrons upstairs."

Lord Shaw was watching Roth, as if expecting shock or dismay at the turn of the conversation.

"A wise approach," Roth replied. "I am pleased to see your family honors its traditions."

Lord Shaw stared at him.

A tiny hand slipped into his, and Roth started. Lady Audra beamed up at him. "I like him," she announced to her brothers. "We should tell him about the—"

"No," Lord Shaw snapped. "Ignore her, Mr. Roth. She's just a girl."

Lady Audra pulled back her hand and stomped a foot. "You take that back!"

"Well, you *are* a girl," Master James pointed out. "There's nothing to be done about that."

"But I'm not *just* a girl!" Lady Audra protested. "I'm a Westerbrook, same as you."

"You are not all Alldenes?" Roth asked, glancing among them. "This is Alldene Castle. Your mother is the Countess of Alldene."

"My mother is a countess in her own right," Lord Shaw said as if he had had to explain the situation entirely too many times. "Our father is—was—a plain master."

"Like me," his brother said proudly.

"I have her courtesy title," Lord Shaw explained. "I'm her heir."

Roth would have thought that would bring the lad's head back up again, but it had sagged. So had his shoulders, as if entirely too many matters were riding on them.

Matters Roth would have to help him find a way to carry. Perhaps this position was more important than he'd thought.

After Meredith and her pet had departed, Thea had tried to settle back in at the desk in the upstairs library. Her neighbor, Mrs. Winfield, had invited her to tea. She would refuse as she refused most such courtesies. She had entirely too much to do.

She had to determine what they would plant on the home farm below the castle to the north this spring and decide whether they had sufficient sheep and cows for their needs or should seek to purchase additional animals.

It was also time for the quarterly review of their investments in the Exchange. She wasn't too sure about the shares in shipping Thomas had been so keen on.

Thank goodness he had not fallen for the Poyais scandal that had sent many of its investors to Debtors' Prison. She would not support slave-worked plantations in Jamaica, despite the excellent returns on sugar. There had to be something worthwhile in which she could put her excess funds. Though perhaps she should be holding onto those funds. She had a report from the Scotland estate that some of the roofs on the tenant cottages would not last the winter.

Indeed, it was rare that she ever saw the teak of the desk under the mountain of papers demanding her attention.

How had Father managed it?

She sighed. Her father had been the consummate earl, always prepared, always ready with a swift decision. He hadn't even needed to consult the many tomes filling the glass-fronted bookshelves between the windows. Had he ever parted the thick emerald velvet draperies and gazed out at his holdings, wondering which would need his attention next?

"An earl must be the master of many things, Thea," he'd told her. "You must give the matters that come before you your full attention."

That might have been easier for him. He had had only one child, with a nursery maid, nurse, and later governess, and her mother to oversee them all. While she had a nurse and nursery maid, she had three children. With Thomas gone, their upbringing fell entirely on her shoulders.

And she wouldn't have had it any other way.

Felden slipped into the room and padded over to the hearth. It was the footman's task to make sure the coal was sufficient, but after Thomas's death, her butler had begun to take responsibility for whatever room she happened to enter.

She leaned back in her curved teak chair. "Did the children return Mr. Roth to the schoolroom in one piece?"

The red glow of the fire illuminated Felden's smile as he shook a few more pieces of coal from the brass scuttle. "I don't believe they've reached it yet, your ladyship. There is a great deal of castle to show the fellow."

Thea glanced at the ormolu clock on the corner of the desk. It was the one concession to her own tastes she'd allowed in the masculine room. The Grecian maiden teetering at the top of the piece, her flowered skirts supported by cherubim, looked far more relaxed than she felt.

Had two hours really passed? It was a big castle, as she had cause to know from her childhood rambles and her upkeep of it as an adult, but surely Mr. Roth would have directed them into something more purposeful by now. Had he no interest in setting up his lodgings? In organizing the schoolroom?

Or had she chosen the wrong tutor after all?

She caught herself nibbling on a nail and dropped her hand. Rising, she nodded to Felden. "I believe I'll go see how they're getting along."

The schoolroom lay on the top story, with the tutor's or governess's quarters at one end. Like the rest of the house, it had been paneled in dark wood, but her mother had insisted on painting it a buttery yellow. Now the two gable windows poured light onto the polished wood floor, the sturdy worktable in the center of the room, and the low shelves of books and slates and globes and all manner of things any growing child might need to learn.

But not one child was in sight, and no one answered her rap at either of her sons' rooms or the tutor's.

The nursery lay on the other side of the stairs. Though the fire sent a warm glow through the cozy, carpeted space, Audra was not there to appreciate it. Neither was Nurse Waters. Thea rapped on the nurse's room at the back of the nursery.

Waters whipped open the portal, face a scowl. Meeting Thea's gaze, she hastily bowed her head and dropped a curtsey. "Your ladyship. How might I be of assistance?"

"Where are the children?" Thea asked. "I can't locate them."

She rose, scowl still in place, but this time, Thea thought, it was directed at her new colleague. "With that tutor, I imagine. He doesn't strike me as very trustworthy, if you don't mind my saying, your ladyship. A soldier? What's he going to do? Make them march up and down the corridors all day? Lady Audra already spends entirely too much time trying to ape her brothers." She leaned closer, and Thea caught a whiff of gardenias. "She told me she wants to wear trousers!"

"I'll speak to her about the matter," Thea promised, removing herself from the cloying scent. "And I will send her back to you as soon as I find them."

She tried to walk with confidence and grace back down the corridor, but her feet were moving entirely too fast. Highwaymen had been captured only recently after trying to kidnap Miss Julia Hewett. They'd attacked several carriages before then. And what of the train robbery? It had taken three Imperial Guards to subdue the villains. Was Mr. Roth up to the task of caring for her children alone? Had her decision put Shaw, James, and Audra in danger?

She fled down to the chamber story and swept from room to room, but outside of startling a few maids at work, she found no one. She should enlist Felden or the footmen to search. She could almost hear Thomas's scold.

"Such haste is not in keeping with the status of a countess, my dear," he'd say as she'd hurry into the dining room to join him. "Your staff and tenants must see someone in command, or you will have a very difficult time of it."

Her father had said similar things when she was growing up. Skipping about the courtyard was for lesser beings, and heaven forbid that she run along the ramparts, wind streaming through her hair. She was his only child, his heir, the person on whom the entire future rested. She must be calm, composed, fearless at all times.

So why was fear clawing at her now?

"Have you seen Mr. Roth and the children?" she asked Hartshorn, the newer footman, who was on duty by the door. A dark-haired fellow with sharp blue eyes, he stood taller, cleft chin quivering only slightly.

"They went outside some time ago, your ladyship."

Even his response seemed to question her judgment!

And who could blame him? The sun might be shining, but the day was still cold. On the other hand, a constitutional could be bracing. The children were often confined to the house for days. Was it truly a bad thing that they were outside?

Either way, she'd feel better if she knew what they were doing.

"Fetch my cloak and gloves," she told her footman.

A few moments later, she was out into the courtyard. Her heart was thudding in her ears, but she forced herself to stop, to listen. Were they near at hand, or had he taken them down the hill toward the village?

Debris brought in by the wind scraped against the grey stones. Carter, her head footman, should be keeping up with sweeping. She would have to have a word with Felden about that.

A shutter creaked in the breeze. She should speak to Wilson, her groundskeeper, about oiling them.

Why did something always need doing!

"Shaw! You almost hit that duck!"

Audra! She looked up and gasped as her daughter's lithe figure flashed past an opening in the stone.

He had them on the ramparts?

She lifted her skirts and dashed into the corner tower, following the curving stair up, up, up, until it opened onto the walkway running between it and the entry tower. The cold wind caught at her. Roth stood, arms crossed over his impressive chest, while both James and Shaw leaned out over the moat.

"What are you doing!" she cried, stalking up to them. "Shaw, James, get away from there immediately."

Both her sons put their feet firmly back on the walk and clasped their hands behind their backs. A stone clicked against the rampart as it tumbled from James's fingers.

"Is there a reason the children should not be here?" Mr. Roth had the audacity to ask.

Thea rounded on him. "Of course there is! They might fall!"

Audra went skipping past, and he grabbed her by the back of her gown and pulled her to a stop.

"I have the matter in hand," he said. She could barely breathe with the anger pulsing through her. Had the man no sense? No sensibilities? "So I see."

He gently nudged Audra closer to her. "Perhaps you might take your daughter inside, where it is warm. "

"She would be perfectly warm if you'd thought to have her don a coat," she informed him. All three of them had red noses, and she would not have been surprised to find their fingers turning blue.

She focused on Shaw and James, the latter of whom was shuffling his feet as if waiting for his turn to be chastised. "Boys, return to the nursery this minute, and take Audra with you. Waters is waiting."

Audra cast her a pouting glance, as if she was very disappointed in her. James dropped his head and started for the stairs. Shaw strolled along as if pleased with himself.

Had he engineered this to give his new tutor a poor showing?

Or had she hired a tutor she couldn't trust with her children?

CHAPTER THREE

HE WASN'T SURE why she was so concerned. It hadn't rained recently, so the stones weren't slippery. The towers on either end of the walk sheltered the children for the most part from the wind. The lip of the parapet rose well into their chests so that it would be difficult for them to tip over it. And he had been watching every moment.

Yet, now freed from the mask of her black veil, those blue eyes crackled with emotion, and she had paled. Was she so angry?

No, she was panicked. Why?

"Is there some danger to the children I should be aware of?" he asked.

She drew an audible breath and gathered her dignity around her like a coronation robe. "No. Just see that you are more sensible in future."

With a swirl of her cloak, she left him.

He glanced out at the countryside again. From here, he could see the slope down to the village, the glint of the river where it flowed through the fields. A few cottages clung to the churchyard, and there seemed to be one or two shops as well. The villagers would have to travel to Weybridge for better or make it all themselves.

He was well acquainted with danger. He saw none here. She clearly did, and he did not doubt her. What was he missing?

The children had only shown him a portion of the castle, so he took some time to go over the rest. Each wing of the house had three floors, with a basement underlying the central portion. The east wing of the ground floor held the kitchen and quarters for the upper servants. The first floor mostly consisted of bedchambers, along with a breakfast room and a library. The west wing and central portion of the top story were largely for the children, although the large practice room with various armaments must have been devised by her father or late husband. He had to stop himself from taking up one of the swords and giving it a swing.

The east wing of the upper floor accounted for the rest of the staff quarters. He did not notice an empty chamber for him among them. The basement even held rooms with stout iron bars. The space was being used to store extra chairs and trunks, but it had clearly once been a dungeon. Might come in handy.

He chuckled to himself as he climbed the stairs back into the main part of the house. If Lady Alldene had been terrified her children might be hurt playing on the ramparts, she was unlikely to endorse his use of the dungeon for discipline.

When he was satisfied he had a good understanding of the place, he hunted up Mr. Felden and requested to be shown to his room. The butler himself escorted him back to the top story.

"The boys could use a gentleman of your talents," Felden told him. "The previous tutor was, if I may be so bold, a rather timid sort."

Roth snorted. "That will not be my problem."

"No, I quite agree." Felden grinned at him.

"You are an odd butler," Roth said.

Standing taller, Felden gazed at Roth with narrowed eyes. "You will not speak to me that in manner. I am your superior."

Roth clapped his fist to his chest and inclined his head. "Forgive my impertinence."

Felden started laughing. "You should see the look on your face. I have never become accustomed to being the uppermost servant around here. You'll find I rule with a very soft glove."

"As you say," Roth allowed, bemused, as he lowered his arm.

"And here you go," Felden said, motioning to the door at the very end of the corridor, past the schoolroom. "The tutor's quarters."

Roth glanced into the room. Someone had painted the paneling a very pleasant blue and provided a large bed hung with chintz patterned in geometric shapes. There was a large wardrobe, a small desk, and a suitable washstand with a porcelain bowl. It was nicer than he'd expected.

"Where do Lord Shaw and Master James sleep?" he asked.

Feldon nodded down the corridor in the opposite direction. "They have their own bedchambers next door to each other just there. Lady Audra and Nurse Waters are on the other side of the stairs."

Roth straightened. "Then this won't do. I need to be between the boys and the stairs."

Felden's brows rose. "Oh, clever. There is another room between Lord Shaw's and the stairs, but it was meant more for a dressing room. It's half the size of this one."

"If it can hold a bed, a trunk for my things, and a washstand, that's all I need," Roth assured him.

"Then I'll have it made up for you over dinner."

"I understood I would eat with the staff," Roth said as they turned from the door.

Felden shook his head. "I am certain Lady Alldene said you were to eat with the family."

That should make for an interesting dinner.

"In that case," Roth said, rubbing a chin where stubble was beginning to form, "I would appreciate somewhere to clean up first."

Dinner was apparently served early here, for Felden advised him to be in the dining room by a quarter to six. Roth discovered it to be a stately room. Only three of the walls were paneled, all the way to the ceiling this time, but the fourth boasted windows flanking a massive stone hearth sculpted with successive bands of flowers, grain, and grapes and surmounted by a tapestry of knights hunting a stag. He had only a moment to take in the grandeur before the countess entered.

She apparently followed the custom of dressing for dinner, for this black gown was frosted with lace, and jet beads sparkled near the high collar. Her eyes widened for a moment, as if she were surprised to find him still in her home, then she glided to the upholstered chair at the top of the table. "Mr. Roth. I'm glad you could join us."

He moved without thinking, beating the footman to the chair by several steps to pull it out for her. "Your ladyship."

She sat without looking at him.

He counted the place settings on the long table. Surely the ones closest to her were reserved for her children. He took the one farthest away.

Voices from the corridor announced the children's arrival. Nurse Waters ushered her charges into the room like a mother hen her chicks. She fluffed up her feathers at the sight of Roth at the table, but flounced over to sit beside Lady Audra.

"You're still here," Lady Audra proclaimed.

Roth fought a smile. "I hope to be here for some time to come."

Lord Shaw laughed and turned the sound into a cough as his mother glanced his way.

Dinner consisted of a main course and a dessert course. He had heard Prince Otto Leopold extol the Salmis de Perdrix the English served, so he recognized the nice mess of chopped partridge, ham, vegetables, mushrooms, and herbs that was served along with buttered broccoli and parsnips. Lady Audra, who was across the table from him, did not seem nearly as delighted, for she picked at the hash, and Master James, on his left, carefully separated the mushrooms from the rest and left them on his plate.

Roth ate it all. Even after years of living with the king and his sons, he still remembered a time when he hadn't been sure when the next meal was coming.

"And what have you decided about the curriculum, Mr. Roth?" the countess asked after chatting with her sons and daughter.

Roth swallowed his bite of parsnip. "We will start the morning with physical exercise—a brisk walk if the weather is good, strengthening exercises if not. Then we will work on history, mathematics, and natural philosophy. After a break for sustenance, we will attack literature and languages, followed by alternating practice with sword and fisticuffs."

Master James's eyes were round. "May I really use a sword?"

"A practice sword," his mother answered with a look to Roth. "I'm sure we have some around with blunted tips."

Roth inclined his head. "I saw some upstairs, your ladyship."

Lord Shaw was watching him. "Languages, you say? What sorts of languages would you know?"

"Shaw," his mother said, warning in the tone.

"I speak, read, and write fluent English, French, and German," Roth replied. "I know a smattering of Italian as well." Mostly for forbidding entry, ordering food, and asking where to find the retiring room, but they didn't need to know that.

"Lord Westerbrook says I must know Latin and Greek," Lord Shaw complained to his mother. "I'll be behind the rest of the students otherwise."

"The vicar can tutor you in those subjects next year," Lady Alldene replied, neatly cutting a parsnip in two. "And you won't be behind anyone, Shaw. I told you, I have no intention of sending you to Eton."

The boy drove his fork into his hash and left it there.

Lady Alldene turned her attention to Roth again. "Your curriculum sounds fairly well rounded, though I wonder about music and the arts."

Roth regarded her. "Does a gentleman need to know such things?"

"I play the piano," Master James put in. "Father taught me."

"You plunk at it," Lord Shaw reminded him. "You don't actually play, at least, not any tune I recognize."

His brother colored.

"I don't want to learn to play the piano," Lady Audra announced. "I want to hit things with my fist." She smacked one hand into the other as if to demonstrate.

"Nonsense," her nurse scolded her, her cheeks darkening. "Ladies have no need to use their fists, for any purpose. They have gentlemen to protect them."

"I'm not sure fisticuffs would be wise at this point, Audra," her mother said, "though it's always good if a lady knows how to protect herself as well. There are times when no gentleman is handy or willing."

They all applied themselves to their dinners then.

Interesting. Had her husband been unwilling or unable to assist her?

"If you provide me with a list of subjects you would like to introduce, Lady Alldene," he said, "I will do whatever I can to see your sons schooled in them."

That smile. It stopped his movement, his very breath.

"Thank you, Mr. Roth," she said, and he felt as if he were the bravest, wisest man to ever live.

And that was very dangerous indeed.

A gentleman who listened. How very refreshing.

Immediately Thea scolded herself. Thomas had listened. Often with a wry smile and a quick wit to point out the error in her thinking, but still. And Felden listened to her instructions and occasionally did something the exact opposite, all with a self-effacing explanation that was perfectly logical and made her wonder why she hadn't seen the proper approach in the first place.

Roth merely accepted her request and promised to implement it. She could not help being satisfied in that, although she would need to check that he was as good as his word.

They adjourned to the withdrawing room as was their habit after dinner. Nurse Waters took up a chair in the corner. Roth eyed her, then found a similar spot in the opposite corner. The boys settled on either side of the chess board for their ongoing match. Thea took the opportunity to pull her daughter closer.

"What's this I hear about you insisting on wearing trousers?" she asked.

Audra's face took on a mulish cast. "Shaw and James are in long pants. It's much easier for them to crawl about the castle."

Shaw glanced up and shook his head. Audra slumped.

"You have no need to crawl anywhere," Thea reminded her, cuddling her closer and relishing the crisp lemon scent of her. "But if your clothes feel too close, we can expand the skirts to give you more room to move."

Audra beamed at her. "Thank you, Mother. That will help a lot when I take up the sword."

The idea of a blade, even one with a blunted tip, in her little girl's hand chilled her blood. "I believe we agreed you would not fence with your brothers, Audra."

"Why?" she begged. "I'm smart. I'm strong."

Thea brushed a curl back from her daughter's forehead. "You are smart, and you are strong. But you are also smaller than they are. It wouldn't be safe for you."

"So, when I'm bigger?" Audra asked, gaze searching hers.

"When you're bigger, we can discuss the matter again," Thea promised. "Just remember, darling, that you will likely always be smaller than your brothers, even when you are full-grown."

Audra dropped her gaze and muttered something under her breath. Thea decided not to press or admonish. She might have been an only child, but she remembered all too well the things she had had to forego for the dignity of a countess.

All too soon, the clock struck eight, and Nurse Waters rose to take the children to bed. Roth stood as well.

"Goodnight, my loves," Thea said, giving each of her children a hug in turn. Audra pressed against her, James laid his head against her chest, and even Shaw suffered his turn. She watched as Nurse Waters led them from the room, already wanting to call them back.

"You will keep them safe," she said to Roth as he made to follow.

He stopped, turned, and pressed his fist to his chest, gaze meeting hers. "On my honor, I promise, Lady Alldene."

Strength she hadn't known flowed through her, along with an assurance that everything would be all right. Unable to speak, she nodded, and he quit the room.

And the room felt entirely too empty in his absence.

She shook herself. It wasn't him she was missing, but Thomas. Thomas, who could charm away her doubts and fears. Thomas, who knew how to get Audra to comply with only a smile. Thomas, who had helped her think through every difficult decision after the death of her father and her elevation to the title.

But Thomas was by her side no more. Everything was on her shoulders now.

Even dealing with his loathsome cousin.

She would never understand why her husband had made Lord Westerbrook the guardian of their sons in his will unless she should marry again. She and Thomas had disagreed over having the boys sent away to school, but hadn't he trusted her to see to their upbringing in his absence? As it was, Viscount Westerbrook arrived on a whim from time to time to wreak havoc in her life, all in the name of being a proper guardian.

The next day was no different. Thea had just settled in on a plan to expand the orchard when Felden announced the viscount. She set her work aside and went down to the withdrawing room to receive him but couldn't seem to find even a polite smile as he strutted into her company as if he owned her castle.

"Thea, dear," he said, coming forward with outstretched hands.

She shuddered. Perhaps it was his golden good looks, from his artfully combed blond hair to the satin-striped waistcoat on his manly chest. Perhaps it was the way he smiled so complacently. Perhaps it was merely the fact that he never called her by her title, even though her status was above his.

She rose and went to the hearth to avoid the peck on her cheek. "Westerbrook. What brings you out this way?"

Until recently, it had been to see Miss Julia Hewett, whom he had been courting. Thea was glad that young lady had decided on another gentleman, one of Roth's fellow guardsman, Mr. Tanner.

"Why, I came to see my wards, of course," Westerbrook said, going to sit on the closest sofa and leaning against the back as if he had no regard for the fact that she was still standing. "Where are the little darlings?"

Shaw would have been mortified to be called little, in any use of the word. "They are at lessons with their new tutor."

His face brightened. "Ah, then you took my advice about preparing them to enter Eton."

"I took your advice to find them a proper tutor," she amended. "I have decided against sending them away."

He shook his head. "Thea. You know it is expected of a gentleman. You cannot coddle them forever."

For as long as possible, she could. "There is much Shaw must learn about taking on the title one day," she temporized. "He can do that best here."

"And this tutor," Westerbrook said, tone flattening as if he were already bored, "is he of the same caliber as the last, which, I must say, was sadly lacking?"

Thea allowed herself a smile. "No, he is of a different temperament and schooling entirely. A former military man, a stern disciplinarian, as you suggested."

"Excellent." He crossed his boots at the ankles. "Send for him. I'd like to meet him."

She debated doing as he asked, but it didn't seem fair to Roth to have to deal with the viscount's shock. "But you've already met him. Mr. Stephen Roth, the last of Lady Belfort's Imperial Guards."

Red flushed into his face, and he surged to his feet. "No. Out of the question. You will discharge him immediately."

Her heart sped, but she merely took a seat. "Why, Westerbrook, such vehemence. What about Mr. Roth could so incense you? He seems rather benign to me."

"Because you have no understanding," he said, beginning to pace before her like a caged tiger. "This sort of poor decision making is exactly why Alldene felt the need to name me as guardian for your sons."

Thea rose slowly, deliberately, refusing to allow him to

see her trembling. "*I* am Alldene. You would be wise to remember that, my lord."

He waved a hand. "A mistaken phrase, no more than that. Surely you see the inadvisability of hiring a fellow who is little more than a foot soldier."

"The King of Batavaria trusted Mr. Roth with his life and the lives of his sons," she informed him. "He has served with distinction, I'm told. That you would diminish him says more about your consequence than his."

His chest rose and fell as if he were panting. "I will not stand for this. You will remove him from this castle before my next visit, or I will have no choice but to remove your sons instead."

CHAPTER FOUR

THEY WERE PLOTTING something.

Roth watched as James and Shaw sat with him in the schoolroom, heads down, scribbling on slates, allegedly working out the mathematical problems he had provided. He had hoped the work might help him determine how much the boys already knew. But at least part of the time, he was fairly certain they were not working on arithmetic.

For one thing, Shaw kept writing and then tapping his chalk against the table. James would peer over and nod.

"No copying," Roth had warned the first time.

Shaw had erased what he'd written with a rag. "Of course not, Mr. Roth."

When James tapped his chalk against the table a short time later, Roth had made a point of strolling past, but the only thing on the boy's slate was the number twelve.

"That is not the correct answer," he told James, who hastily wiped away the number.

Then again, this wasn't the first time he'd caught them at mischief. Felden had been true to his word and outfitted the little room at the head of the stairs with a narrow but comfortable bed, trunk, and washstand. Last night, Roth had kept his door open. He'd always been a light sleeper, so the furtive steps tiptoeing past had woken him instantly.

"Is there a problem, boys?" he'd called, even as he'd risen and gone to the door.

Shaw and James had stared at him, candleholder trembling in Shaw's hand.

"No, sir," he had said. "James just couldn't sleep, so I thought a walk might be beneficial."

James turned his stare on his brother.

"I will speak to your valet," Roth had told them. "He should know better than to allow you to go to bed fully clothed."

James had washed red.

"No need," Shaw had said stiffly. "I will inform Dumart of your concern. Come along, James. It's time for bed."

The two had shuffled back down the corridor. Roth had remained in the doorway until he had heard nothing further.

What was so important that they needed to sneak out? Shaw did not seem the type to court trouble, unless it was discrediting Roth in some way. And James lacked the courage to start trouble on his own.

"Good morning," Lady Alldene called, sailing into the room now. Her black veil was once more in place, fluttering about her as she moved. "How are matters progressing?"

The words were as bright as the sun coming through the windows, but one hand picked at the material of her fine black gown.

"I answered the same questions as Shaw, Mother," James announced, lifting his slate for her to see.

"They were far too easy," Shaw complained.

"Then I'm sure Mr. Roth can devise more challenging ones," she said with a smile his way.

"Once I am certain where the boys' skills lie," he allowed.

Shaw pushed his slate away. "Far beyond this drivel."

"Shaw," his mother warned.

Roth glanced down at the slate. "Interesting. Is that why you answered problem three incorrectly?"

The boy stiffened and yanked the slate closer. "What do you mean? That's the right answer!"

"Is it?" Roth challenged.

"Perhaps if you showed him," his mother started.

Roth held up a hand. "Well, Lord Shaw?"

The boy squinted at the problem, then the slate, then his brow cleared. "Ah, I see." He rubbed out the answer and added a new one, then swiveled the slate for Roth to see. "Correct now?"

"Perfect," Roth said. "Nicely done."

Shaw grinned a moment before schooling his face.

"Are mine right?" James asked, glancing between his brother and Roth.

Roth looked over the answers. "Correct, Master James. Nicely done to you too."

James leaned back and beamed. "And I had them all correct on the first try."

Shaw bumped him with his shoulder. "I would have had them all correct the first time if you hadn't kept distracting me."

"If you are having difficulty managing them both, I could provide some suggestions," Lady Alldene put in.

"No difficulty," Roth said. He pulled a book from the stack on the table. "This is about the War with the Colonies. Begin reading at page ten, and I will return in a moment to see what you make of it."

Shaw frowned as if he wasn't sure what Roth was about, but he accepted the book and bent his head over it. James slid closer and began reading as well, lips moving as he must have sounded out words.

Roth tipped his head to one side and moved closer to the windows. The countess joined him.

"Have I given you reason to doubt me?" he asked.

She leaned her hands on the window sill and directed

her gaze out over the countryside beyond the castle walls. The veil left shadows like lace across her cheeks.

"No, Mr. Roth," she said. "I know you will educate my sons. It's simply that I have more experience with them than you do. I thought that might prove helpful."

"Here is what I have gleaned," Roth said. "Lord Shaw feels the pressure of being your heir. With his father gone, he is attempting to lead. But Master James and Lady Audra resent his leadership, which frustrates him. Master James is unsure of his position. He is keen to please, to the point where he sometimes allows his brother to persuade him into doing something he would otherwise find objectionable. And Lady Audra has spent enough time with her brothers that she struggles to understand why she cannot do everything they can."

Her fingers gripped the sill. "You understand them better than I do!"

There was pain behind that confession. "I am trained to observe and react," he explained. "But you are correct that I was not trained to deal with children. Your insights would be appreciated. Just remember, you hired a man you respected. It would be better for us both if you did not question every decision I make."

She drew in a breath. "But if you're wrong, sir, think of the consequences to my children."

"There are consequences to any decision," he told her. "All we can do is our best, changing tactics as the need becomes apparent."

She met his gaze, her own haunted. "Lord Westerbrook was here earlier. He did not react well when he heard you were the new tutor."

Roth watched her. "You must have known that might be a danger. He has made no secret of his contempt for Mr. Tanner after losing Miss Hewett's regard."

"I knew how he felt about the Imperial Guards. I had hoped that he would find you intimidating enough he would leave off his threats. Instead, he told me that if I don't discharge you, he would return and take the boys by force."

Roth raised his chin. "I would like to see him try."

Her mouth twitched as if she were fighting a smile. "Alas, the law may be on his side. Few have prevailed in Chancery Court, where such matters are tried. When Shaw reaches the age of four and ten, he can petition to have Westerbrook removed as his guardian. I'm less sure about my chances of doing the same before then unless I marry again."

And the matter weighed on her. He could see it in the way her gaze refused to land, the way her hands plucked at her skirts again. Like her son, she carried too many burdens.

"Then I will leave," he said. "I am no good to you if I threaten all you hold dear."

She peered up at him at last. "Are you unhappy in this position?"

Less and less every moment he was in her company. "No. But I cannot add to your burdens."

"You don't," she said. "In fact, I begin to believe you are the only one who can help me shoulder them."

As if she thought she'd said too much, she straightened. "Continue your work, Mr. Roth. You obviously know what you're about. Leave Lord Westerbrook to me."

Sunday morning, Thea sat at her dressing table as her maid, Martin, took the brush to her hair.

"How will you have it this morning, my lady?" she asked, gazing hopefully at Thea's reflection in the mirror.

"Just pull it back out of the way," Thea said.

Martin sighed.

Poor thing. Martin had been with her since Thea had graduated from the schoolroom and had delighted in building complicated braids and curls that set off Thea's lean features to perfection. There had seemed little point in the charade since Thomas had died. No one in the castle cared how she wore her hair, and she would only be draping it in a black veil when she went out or entertained visitors.

She had the veil on when she ventured downstairs a short while later to meet the children in the entry hall for the drive to services. Nurse Waters had prevailed upon Audra to wear one of her prettier dresses, a rose-colored taffeta with flounces at the hem, but her daughter kept eyeing Shaw and James in their long trousers as if still envious.

All three were so quiet as the carriage left the courtyard that she could hear the hooves clattering over the drawbridge. The wooden planks had never been lifted in her lifetime. No danger had been so great they must shelter inside. But she caught herself smiling as she envisioned Lord Westerbrook's face should he arrive next time to find the castle prepared for a siege against him.

"What shall we do this afternoon?" she asked them as the carriage turned into the village. Villagers bundled in coats and cloaks were hurrying toward the church, a few red mittens bright against the stones of the buildings.

"Mr. Roth will probably have us studying," Shaw said heavily.

"Nonsense," Thea told her oldest. "It's the Lord's Day. Besides, Mr. Roth is supposed to have this afternoon off from his duties."

James nudged his brother.

Shaw nodded quickly, then smiled at her. "He deserves time off for all his good work, but James and I still have books to read to meet his requirements. You and Audra can enjoy the time together."

She glanced at her daughter beside her to find Audra's eyes narrowing.

"I'm coming too," she declared.

Thea looked to Shaw. "Coming? Coming where?"

"To the schoolroom, of course," Shaw said with a quelling look to his sister. "Where else would we go?"

Where else indeed?

She had no time to question them further, as the carriage had stopped. The footman came to lower the step and assist them all out in front of St. Pancras at Alldene. The builders who had constructed the castle walls had designed the church as well, with the same eye for defense, for the bell tower in the center of one side was square, a full six stories tall, speckled with slit windows suitable for firing arrows, and surmounted with a cross that one had to squint to see. The other, arched windows looked oddly out of place on the long building.

"Good morning, milady," the deacon said at the door, head respectfully bowed as they entered.

"Good morning," Thea replied, shepherding her children into the chapel. At least someone had prevailed against the dark wood that permeated the castle. The box pews were of a more golden tone with carved finials. They spanned both sides of a center aisle, starting under the sweeping white stone arches that held up the galleries on either side. As a child, she'd imagined King Arthur being crowned at the golden wood altar with its triple crosses and stained-glass windows behind.

More heads bowed in her direction as she and the children progressed up the aisle to the two pews that had belonged to her family for generations. Squire Winfield and his wife, their closest neighbors to the east. The widowed Mrs. Latterly and her daughter, gentry who lived on the west. Thea and the children took the first pew, and her upper staff, including Felden, Mrs.

Willoughby, her housekeeper, and Nurse Waters, took the second. She cast a quick glance back, but she caught no sign of Roth.

Odd. Did he not attend services? Lady Belfort had made it a point to give him the opportunity.

"Was Mr. Roth ill this morning?" she whispered to Shaw on the other side of her from Audra.

"No," he whispered back.

James nodded to the gallery on their left. "He's there, with the footman and grooms."

Glancing up, she saw that he was right. Roth sat, head a good few inches higher than any around him, coat sharp, face serene. A few of the female staff around him were darting glances his way. He kept his gaze on the altar.

Thea hastily returned her gaze to her children.

But she couldn't help noticing other families around them. Husbands and wives shared smiles. Good friends nodded in greeting. The only nods she received were in obeisance or curiosity. What she wouldn't give for a friend.

Once more, her gaze traveled up into the gallery, only to find Roth gazing down at her. For a moment, she thought she saw admiration. Face flaming, she rose with the others as the service started.

The vicar, Mr. Bloomsberg, gave one of his quiet sermons, to the point that she could hear someone behind them snoring before being shushed. He had been the vicar since she was a child, appointed by her father. When he retired, she would have to find his replacement. Perhaps someone with a little more pepper.

"And so we would be wise to continue preparing this holy season of Advent," he finished, "and remember that soon, our hope will appear in the form of a baby on Christmas."

Christmas. Her first since losing Thomas last January. He'd loved to decorate the castle from one end to the other with evergreen boughs, holly, and ivy. How was she to find the heart for it?

How was she to find the time for it?

Rain had begun to fall as they exited the church. It pattered down on the stones of the walkway, darkening them from grey to black. Even Mrs. Winfield and Mrs. Latterly, who loved to chat, did not linger to gossip. Thea hurried the children toward the waiting carriage.

"But Mr. Roth will get wet!" Audra protested, resisting Thea's tug on her arm.

"Soldiers don't mind a little rain," Shaw scoffed.

"Nurse Waters found a ride," James pointed out as they reached the carriage.

Their nurse was indeed climbing up into a carriage with the family of the local physician, who was a distant cousin. Likely she was starting her own half-day off. The rest of Thea's staff were waiting inside the opening to the bell tower, clearly hoping for a break in the weather before starting the climb up to the castle. Thea found her seat with the children in the carriage, then asked Griggs, one of her footmen, to leave the door open and beckoned Felden closer.

Her butler clapped his short-crowned hat tighter to his head and jogged to meet her. "Your ladyship?"

"Send Mr. Roth to me," she told him. "And ask the rest to wait here. I'll have the other carriages return for you."

"Very kind of you, your ladyship," Felden said.

She had just settled herself on the seat beside Audra when the carriage shook. Roth pulled himself inside and hesitated, both hands braced on the opening.

Thea quickly transferred Audra into her lap and motioned James across. Roth took his place beside Shaw on the backward-facing seat as the carriage started out.

"Thank you for thinking of me," he said, lowering a damp collar he had obviously turned up against the rain. A few drops landed on Shaw, who frowned.

"I wouldn't want you to start your afternoon off soaked to the skin," Thea told him.

He leaned back against the squabs. "I had thought to forego my time off this week in hopes of having Tuesday afternoon off instead. My colleague, Mr. Tanner, is marrying."

"Ah, yes," Thea said. "Miss Hewett, his intended, invited me as well. We can take the coach."

He nodded, but immediately something tingled through her. Why? It was only practical that they go together. She shouldn't feel as if she'd agreed to go driving with a suitor.

"Oh, good," Audra said. "If you're going to be in the castle, Mr. Roth, you can come too."

This again? "Where exactly are you going?" Thea asked her daughter.

"Nowhere," Shaw insisted, glaring at his sister. "James and I will be studying. Audra will be with Nurse Waters."

Audra pouted.

"Such studious young men you are developing, Mr. Roth," Thea said. "I trust lessons are going well."

James nodded, and Shaw directed his gaze out the window.

"Reasonably well," Roth said. "Lord Shaw and Master James are both bright and capable. They should have no trouble entering Oxford or Cambridge when the time comes."

Had he mentioned Eton, she thought she might scream. But, by the time her sons were ready to attend college, she might be ready to let them go.

"All these lands are yours?" he asked with a nod toward the window.

"From the River Wey to the Bourne," she explained. "Father used to say anywhere you can walk in half a day."

He raised his brows. "That would have covered most of Batavaria. You may be a countess, but you control as much as some who style themselves kings."

And there were days she felt it to her bones.

"The king of England has been relying on the House of Alldene to protect this part of Surrey since Henry V," Shaw put in.

"And what years did he reign?" Roth asked.

Shaw drew himself up. "From 1413 to 1422. He was a general."

"A man who has served in the military usually knows how to lead," Roth mused, "and how to follow." His gaze brushed Thea's, and she wasn't sure which role he intended to take with her. She barely heard the drawbridge rattle as they crossed into the castle.

But she made sure to let the children out first, then accepted Roth's hand to descend to the cobbles herself. "They are up to something," she murmured to him.

He nodded, watching them. "So I noticed. Never fear. I'll keep an eye on them."

"I had every confidence that you would." She started forward, and her boot slipped on the wet stones. A strong arm wrapped around her, keeping her from falling.

He smiled as he set her gently back on her feet. "Careful."

She nodded, breathless. He took her arm and helped her to the door, then bowed and headed up the stairs after the children.

Such confidence. Such composure. Such strength!

Why was she so tempted to lean on it?

CHAPTER FIVE

THE BOYS WERE not amused by his presence. Roth hadn't intended to make anyone uncomfortable. He simply hadn't felt right taking time away. He had never accepted money under false pretenses.

Only stolen it for his own needs.

He pushed the thought away as he listened to his charges. Shaw and James were arguing over which battalions should advance first in their war of lead soldiers, which were currently spread halfway across the schoolroom. They had tried to sneak out last night too. He'd pretended to snore, watching as they tiptoed past. He'd caught up with them in the entry hall.

"Another midnight stroll?" he asked.

James started, then clung to his brother as if seeing a ghost, but Shaw was more determined.

"It is our home," he complained. "We are allowed to walk through it on occasion."

"I would be happy to walk with you," Roth assured him. "During daylight hours. Dark is time to sleep."

With a sigh, the two had trudged back to bed.

"They are not battalions," Roth said now, stacking the books he intended to use the following week on one end of the worktable.

Shaw's head came up, defiance simmering in the blue of his gaze. "They have battalion markings."

"They have company markings," Roth replied, setting

the last book in place. "Battalions generally have a thousand members. You have many soldiers, but not, I think, a thousand to a side."

James looked around as if counting. "He's right, you know. You have three hundred and ninety-two, and I have two hundred and twenty-seven."

"That's nearly a thousand," Shaw argued.

"That's six hundred nineteen in total," James said. "It isn't a thousand together, much less on each side."

Shaw tipped over his general the way Prince Otto Leopold did a piece on a chessboard when he'd lost. "I'm tired of strategy in any event." He rose. "I'm going to see how Audra is doing." He looked pointedly at his brother.

James paled, but nodded, and Shaw stalked out.

James cleared his throat. "Would you care to play chess, Mr. Roth?"

"I never learned," he said. "I have only watched others play."

James scrambled to his feet, grinning. "Then I'll teach you." He motioned Roth over to a board set up under one of the windows overlooking the hillside.

Roth settled into place across from him. The pieces were ebony and ivory, and the board was inlaid with exotic woods. He fingered the second-tallest piece on his side, which was capped with a tiny crown.

"That is your queen," James told him. "She's your best piece. You want to reserve her for important moves."

Like in life. "And this must be her consort," Roth said, moving his hand to the tallest piece, which had a larger crown with a cross on top.

"The king," James agreed. "If I capture him, I win."

"Then why are all the pieces arranged in a line?" Roth demanded with a frown. "They should be positioned to protect the king at all costs." He began better aligning the pieces.

James started giggling. "No, no, no! That's against the rules."

"Sometimes rules must be broken to keep the ones you love safe," Roth countered. He nodded at his new arrangement, men three deep on every side of the king, including behind him. "There. Now try to capture my king. Unless, of course, you'd like to tell me why your brother wants you to distract me."

James had reached for one of the tall, pointy-topped pieces. His fingers trembled. "I'm sure I don't know what you mean."

"You know exactly what I mean," Roth said, tugging a piece with a crenelated top closer to his king and straddling two squares in the process. "You have tried to sneak out two nights in a row, and now your brother intends to take Audra and do whatever it is you wanted to do."

James pulled back his hand. "It's nothing bad."

"It must be against your rules if you seek to do it with no witnesses," Roth pointed out. He crossed his arms over his chest. "Tell me, or I'll envision the worst."

James gazed up at him, blue eyes soulful. "I can't. I promised."

Roth dropped his arms. "One should never break a promise. I will guess, then. You're trysting with a kitchen maid."

James frowned. "What's trysting?"

Right. They were a bit young for that, and they would hardly involve their sister. "You intend to steal the silver."

Now his brows shot up. "No! What would we want with a bunch of spoons and bowls anyway?"

Especially since Shaw would one day inherit all of it. "You have murdered one of the staff and hope to bury the body."

James goggled. "Where do you get these ideas? We would never do any of that!"

Roth spread his hands. "Then you leave me no choice but to appeal to your mother."

"No, please." James bit his lower lip a moment, then relented. "I can't tell you what they're doing, but I can tell you where they're going: the old guard quarters in the main tower."

Roth rose. "Right. Fetch your coat and come with me."

A few moments later, they started down the stairway for the ground floor.

"Shaw won't be pleased," James murmured, trying to keep pace with Roth. "I was supposed to keep you busy."

"I am busy," Roth said, turning on the landing.

Halfway up, hand lifting her dark skirts, Lady Alldene stopped and smiled. "Ah, there you are. I was just coming to see if the children would like to join me for tea." She glanced around him. "Where's Shaw?"

James looked to Roth, clearly panicked.

"We are playing a game of strategy," Roth told her. "Lord Shaw is in the lead with his sister. Master James and I would be wise to follow. When we catch up, I will inform him of your invitation."

Head high, he passed her, James scurrying after. He could feel her gaze following them.

"Thank you," the boy said as they came out into the entry hall.

"You will have to tell her at some point," Roth reminded him, heading for the entrance. The footman on duty, who Felden had told him was named Griggs, opened the door for them, and they stepped out into the cold. The rain had stopped, but shadows crossed the courtyard, leaving it in twilight. A raven flew over, call sharp. James shivered.

As the boy had predicted, they found Shaw and Audra in a room on the first floor of the main tower, which had once held the guards. All weapons had been removed, and it was clear no fire had been kindled in the hearth in many a year. But a bench ran the length of one wall, and stands here and there spoke of where swords and pikes had once been stored for easy retrieval. The space was dimly lit by two slit windows, and the air was as cold as the stones enclosing it.

Shaw and Audra were sitting on the bench, a piece of paper spread between them. The oldest boy glared at James the moment he and Roth entered. "You promised."

"He did not break his promise," Roth said, positioning himself to block the doorway so they could not escape. "He did not divulge your purpose, only your location."

Audra popped up and came to take his hand. "I'm glad you're here. You can share our secret."

"I don't see why that's necessary, Audra," Shaw argued, folding up his paper and tucking it away.

"He made up a story to keep Mother from finding us, Shaw," James said. "And he knows we've been trying to go out at night."

Shaw's mouth wiggled back and forth a moment, then he nodded. "All right. We could use the help." He stood, tilted back his head, and met Roth's gaze. "We are hunting treasure."

"Treasure?" Roth frowned. "You have one of the largest, most well-appointed homes in England. Why would you need treasure?"

"Everyone needs treasure," Audra piped up. "Pretty stones and shiny coins." She smiled dreamily. A dragon likely looked as delighted with the idea.

"Father told Audra that he had left a treasure," Shaw said impatiently. "But he didn't have a chance to tell her where before he…he died." He paused to swallow. "Mother does a very good job managing this house and the earldom, but there are times when she must economize."

"She has to choose," James said as if he thought Roth might not know the term. "Will she fix the barn or one of the tenant houses?"

"Will she spend time with us or work on all those papers?" Audra added. The face she made left no doubt as to which she preferred.

"Precisely," Shaw said. "She wouldn't have to worry so much if we found the treasure."

"And you are certain this treasure is real?" Roth asked. After all, Shaw was more likely to dismiss his sister than partner with her.

"Yes," Shaw said. "I found a note from Father that confirmed as much. Now, will you help us?"

They were all watching him, waiting, hoping. Like their mother, they had taken on a task too big for them. He wasn't sure how this treasure would help Lady Alldene with her burdens, but it might ease theirs to locate it.

Roth inclined his head. "I would be honored."

Shaw nodded, James beamed, and Audra gave his hand a swing.

"However," he said, and Shaw stiffened. "I ask something in return. You will attend to your lessons. We will merely make sure that finding the treasure is one of those lessons."

"That's only fair," Shaw agreed, and James nodded as well.

"Good," Roth said. "For now, your mother seeks your company. This evening, before we retire, you can tell me how you have searched since your father died, and we will develop a plan to find your treasure."

She and Thomas had generally spent Sunday afternoon with the children. They might read stories aloud or play a game. Sometimes they rode out, Thomas and the boys on horseback and she and Audra in a pony cart. She knew Shaw and James had intended to study, but surely they would join her for tea. They enjoyed the sweet treats Mrs. Naughton, their cook, baked as much as Thea did.

But her children had not appeared at the usual time. The nursemaid who had charge of Audra while Nurse Waters was off might have forgotten, but it had dawned on her that Roth might not realize the tradition. So, she had gone in search of them.

Only to find all three children were playing a game with him instead, and she had been dismissed.

She told herself to be pleased her sons were already becoming attached to their tutor. When was the last time Shaw and James had gone willingly to their studies? How her oldest must be relishing a game involving strategy.

But could she not have joined them? Perhaps she should have invited herself. Or would that be infringing on their newfound sense of responsibility?

Oh, why must everything involve impossible decisions!

She had already told Felden to clear away the tea things, having entirely lost her appetite, when her children filed in. Their cheeks were pink, as if they had been out in the cold.

"What were you up to?" she asked her trio as James and Audra came to sit beside her on the sofa. Shaw would once have been right there with them, but he took the chair Thomas had preferred and ran his hands along the arms. Her chest tightened.

Roth settled on the chair in the corner. She almost asked him closer, but decided not to push.

"Playing a game of strategy, like we told you," James answered her, though his face was turning red. "I won."

"No," Shaw said. "I won."

"Shaw always wins," Audra said, but her gaze was on Roth.

Thea did not want to waste precious time arguing.

"Well, it sounds like an interesting game. What shall we do today, the four of us?"

"Let's sing," Audra suggested, hand rubbing at Thea's gown. "You can play the piano."

James scrunched up his face. "I don't like singing. It hurts my ears."

"We aren't that bad," Thea protested with a laugh.

"We aren't that good, either," Shaw said. "You could read to us about the Peloponnesian War. Father said the Greeks were very smart in their strategy."

"Do they use swords?" Audra asked her.

What was it about sharp objects that drew her daughter? "I think I'll save Greek military history for Mr. Roth." She smiled to him.

Audra glanced his way again. "What do you do on Sundays, Mr. Roth?"

"Polish my weapons," he said.

"Well, that will never do," Thea said, laugh bubbling up again. "What about kitty in the corner?"

Shaw rolled his eyes. "Mother, that game is for babies."

"I like it," Audra insisted. "James likes it too." She looked at her brother around Thea. "Don't you, James?"

James glanced between her and Shaw. "Well, I liked it when I was younger."

Couldn't she even introduce a game?

Roth rose. "I do not know this game. Teach it to me."

Oh, bless him! That was all it took for her children to rally themselves and rush to his aid.

"We each take a corner of the room," James explained, "and our cat person stands in the middle."

Audra pushed herself off the sofa. "I want to be the kitty!"

"That would be fine, Audra," Thea said to forestall another argument.

"When Audra says she wants a corner," James continued.

"When kitty wants a corner," Audra interrupted.

"Yes, yes, when kitty says she wants a corner," James allowed, "we must trade places. If she manages to reach a corner before one of us, that person must become the kitty."

"There is a sort of strategy to it," Shaw confided to Roth, who had moved closer. "You and another can switch places, for example." He looked to James, who nodded.

Audra stalked to the center of the room. "Let's play!"

Thea took up a spot in the corner closest to the hearth. Roth was opposite her. She could see his gaze swinging from boy to boy, as if gaging his chances of beating them to a corner.

"Meow," Audra said, pausing to rub a wrist along her cheek.

"What are you doing?" Shaw demanded.

She dropped her hand. "I am a cat! That's what cats do! Didn't you watch Fortune?"

"Just get on with it," he told her.

Audra gave him an arch look that did indeed remind Thea of Meredith's pet. She stifled a giggle.

"Kitty wants a corner!" Audra cried.

James and Shaw took off running. Thea scooted across the room and set herself in the corner her oldest had vacated. Roth was now in James's corner.

And Audra was in Shaw's. She grinned at her oldest brother. "You're the kitty now."

Shaw glowered at her. "Kitty wants a corner!"

James and Audra crossed each other, obviously intending to swap places. Thea raced for the empty corner. So did Roth. They collided in the middle, and his arms came around her, steadying her. Warmth rushed from her toes to her top, and she couldn't look away from that steely gaze.

"Run, Mother!" Audra cried.

Thea shook herself, pulled out of Roth's grip, and dashed for the last empty corner.

Leaving him in the middle.

He stalked to the center of the room, looking far more like a panther than any tabby cat she'd ever seen. He glanced from James to Shaw, then back at Audra.

"Kitty wants a corner!" he boomed.

They all took off running. He caught Audra as she came past and swept her off her feet.

"Not fair!" she cried, wiggling in his arms.

He set her on her feet and ran to the corner she'd vacated.

Only to find Thea there first.

Thea shook her head, giggle escaping. "This corner is taken, Mr. Kitty."

His gaze was wild. "Please. Do not make me be a cat again."

With a laugh, Thea stepped out of her corner. "Oh dear! I appear to be last!"

"But always first in my esteem," Roth assured her, slipping into her place.

She wasn't sure how long they played. For a too brief moment, she forgot all about the decisions waiting for her in the library, Lord Westerbrook's threat, and the impending holiday. It wasn't until Felden came to tell them dinner was going to be served, and the children were starting for the dining room that she realized she hadn't thought of Thomas all afternoon either.

Roth intercepted her before she could follow the children.

"There is something you should know," he murmured.

Her gaze darted to his. What, was she expecting a declaration of admiration? What was wrong with her!

"Yes," she managed, sounding ridiculously breathless.

"The children are in the middle of a treasure hunt.

They believe their father hid something for them. He apparently told Audra as much before his death."

She swallowed. "He never mentioned it to me, but it would be very like Thomas. He enjoyed games. Did you attempt to dissuade them?"

"No," he admitted, glancing after them. "I bargained with them. They attend to their studies, and I will help them search."

She should see this as a distraction, but all she could think was that it was nice her children had the opportunity to be children.

"A very wise course," she said. "Just watch over them. This castle has many odd corners and crevices. I think I explored them all when I was a child."

He smiled, and gooseflesh popped up on her arms. "Perhaps you should join us."

Crawling through dark areas, with him at her side? Not the best choice given these odd whims that had seized her. "I'll leave it to you. But I hope you and the children will share the treasure with me when you find it."

"As far as I am concerned, you are the children's treasure," he said, and he left her there, standing speechless.

CHAPTER SIX

HOW COULD HE not admire such a mother? The Batavarian Queen had been gone by the time Roth had joined the Imperial Guards, and his own mother had died birthing him. Many of the other fine ladies he had guarded over the years at the king's request had left the upbringing of their children to specially trained staff. He'd thought it would be the same here.

Instead, though she had staff to instruct and care for her children, she spent time with them, teaching, encouraging. Even playing.

He smiled as he escorted the children back up to the schoolroom wing after dinner. With her hands fisted in her skirts as she'd darted about the withdrawing room, there had been a fire in Lady Alldene, a joy he had not expected. She might have to act as the stern head of the family for much of the week, but with her children, she could be herself.

And that woman was nothing short of amazing. It was an honor to serve her.

"You are very fortunate in your mother," he told the children as they settled around the worktable. Nurse Waters would be returning some time that evening. The nursery maid who would have had to take charge of Audra had been happy to leave her in his company until it was time for bed.

"Mother is wonderful," Audra said with a contented sigh now as she leaned her elbows on the table.

"She is a credit to her position," Shaw agreed loftily.

"She deserves all our help," James agreed.

Shaw pushed a piece of paper at Roth. "Which is why we need to find that treasure."

Roth pushed it back. "Draw me a map of the castle. Every room, every floor, including the rooms in the fortress wall."

James visibly swallowed. "That's a lot of rooms."

"And we may need to search them all," Roth warned as Shaw began sketching. "Your father left you no clue?"

"He said it was a rich treasure," Audra offered. "He said Mother would want it."

Again he could only wonder why. Lady Alldene appeared to want for nothing except the time to manage her affairs.

James was watching his brother draw. "You forgot the silver cupboard."

Shaw threw down the pencil. "You draw it then!"

James pulled the paper and pencil to him.

"Did the note you found say anything about location?" Roth asked the older boy.

"No," he grumbled. "I don't think he had time to finish the note. It was in the gentlemen's salon, near his sword. It just said, 'I have gathered the treasure, but I am reconsidering.'"

Roth frowned. "Reconsidering what?"

Shaw shrugged. "I don't know. Maybe he was going to add more?"

"He died fast," Audra told Roth, little mouth turned down. "Someone squeezed his heart."

"A seizure of the heart," Shaw corrected her. "It's just something that happens to old people like Mother and Mr. Roth."

He hadn't considered himself old until that moment.

Audra scrambled off the bench. "I don't want Mother's heart to be seized!" Tears dimmed her dark eyes.

Roth put a hand on her tiny shoulder. "Your mother seems in excellent health, Lady Audra."

"Father seemed in excellent health too," James pointed out, drawing the jagged edge of the portcullis on his map. "And then he was gone."

"No!" Audra pulled away from Roth's touch. "Mother won't leave us. You won't leave us either, will you, Mr. Roth?"

The words were more demand than request. Shaw eyed him. James stopped sketching.

"I will do all I can to remain at your side," Roth promised, throat unexpectedly tight. "And I know your mother feels the same way."

That seemed to satisfy James and Audra, for the boy resumed his work and Audra resumed her seat, sliding closer to Roth. Shaw merely focused on his brother's sketches, ignoring Roth.

"What rooms have you already searched?" Roth asked, hoping to get them back on topic.

"Not many," Shaw said. "Mr. Leonard, our previous tutor, kept us too busy during the day, and some of us are afraid of the dark." He looked to his brother.

James frowned at him. "It isn't the dark, and you know it. It's the ghostly footsteps."

"Monsters," Audra whispered, eyes now wide.

Roth glanced from one to the other. "I do not believe in ghosts or monsters."

Shaw nodded. "I tried to tell them, but they wouldn't listen."

Audra leaned against Roth. "You can protect us."

He could indeed. The urge had never felt stronger.

In the end, they decided on a plan to search the remaining rooms, save one. They all agreed that the children's father would have been unlikely to hide anything in their mother's private chambers. Roth was just as glad. It would be hard enough explaining the need to search the wine cellar without having to face the countess as he pawed through her things.

He was equally pleased that Shaw and James attended to their lessons on Monday, leaving them time to begin their search. Audra had insisted on being included, so Roth went to battle with Nurse Waters to see her freed.

"The armory?" she asked, plump nose in the air. "What would Lady Audra possibly learn there?"

"Her country's and family's history," Roth explained. "I promise I will watch her closely, so that no harm comes to her."

Nurse Waters looked skeptical, but Audra was bouncing up and down on her slippers, and the nurse eventually relented.

"And you can show me how to swing a sword," Audra chatted as they headed down to the ground floor. "And how to jab with a pike." She made pushing motions.

"We are searching for treasure," Roth reminded her. "Other pursuits will have to wait."

He was thankful she did not press further.

But though they peered inside every suit of armor, moved aside each shield, and checked every drawer and cupboard, they found nothing Roth would not have expected.

They were coming out of the armory when they heard raised voices from down the corridor.

"I thought I made myself perfectly clear the last time I visited."

James took a step closer to Roth. "That's Lord Westerbrook."

Audra pressed herself against Roth as well, voice hushed. "He sounds angry."

Shaw's fists tightened at his sides. "He should show Mother more respect."

"Agreed," Roth said. "Take your sister back to her nurse, and return to the schoolroom, boys. I will join you in a moment."

James snatched up Audra's hand and led her toward the entry hall, steps so quick it was clear he only wanted to escape.

Shaw hesitated. "He is very good at the sword, but he has a poor right hook. Father beat him at boxing every time."

"I will keep that in mind," Roth said.

With a nod, the boy followed his siblings.

Roth moved swiftly and silently up to the open withdrawing room door, then angled his body so that he could see inside without easily being seen. Lady Alldene was standing near the hearth, chin up and body stiff, while Lord Westerbrook paced in front of her, hands waving.

"Of course he wanted to help with this treasure hunt. He likely hopes to keep the treasure for himself. He is no gentleman, Thea, despite Lady Belfort's patronage. I doubt he has a drop of education. How you can defend him is beyond me."

"Then perhaps," Roth said, stepping into the room. "I should defend myself."

Lord Westerbrook froze, and for one moment, Roth thought he saw fear flicker across his aristocratic face. Then he looked to the countess. "What did I tell you, Thea? Skulking about. Listening at keyholes. This is the man you want tutoring your sons?"

"The door was open," Roth said. "Your voice carried far enough that the children were concerned for their mother's safety." He bowed to Lady Alldene. "Are you well, your ladyship?"

"Better now, Mr. Roth," she said. "Thank you." She turned to Westerbrook. "I have reviewed Mr. Roth's credentials and spoken to those who have employed him in the past. I found nothing to concern me. Since you have not made a similar review, you will have to trust my judgment on the matter."

"Trust your judgment?" he sneered. "Why? Thomas certainly didn't."

She paled.

Roth had had enough. He strode up to the man, who at least had the good sense to take a step back and raise his fists to defend himself. Yet a smile hovered on his thin lips. He wanted Roth to strike him, because that was against the law in England. One blow and Roth could be facing the noose. Lord Westerbrook was willing to risk even a bloody lip if it meant he could rid himself of Lady Alldene's protector.

"These English colleges," Roth said, "do they teach you to prey on women?"

Westerbrook was clearly shocked, for his hands fell. "Certainly not!"

"Ah, then it is a flaw in your own character," Roth surmised. "That is something only you can correct."

The viscount's mouth opened and closed twice before he drew himself up. "You were not invited into this conversation, sir. A gentleman would leave."

"I thought gentlemen only left a lady's presence with her permission," Roth said. Once more he looked to Lady Alldene, who was watching him. "Or am I mistaken?"

"No, indeed, Mr. Roth," she said. "Your manners are impeccable. My sons could not be in better hands."

Lord Westerbrook shook his head. "I disagree, but I see my word carries little weight at the moment. Just make sure that you treat my wards with the respect due them, sir." He bowed. "Thea. If you'll pardon me, I have business in the area."

"Of course," Lady Alldene said, and Roth thought he heard delight in the tone. "Will we see you at Julia Hewett's wedding tomorrow?"

His jaw tightened so fast Roth wouldn't have been surprised to hear a tooth crack. "No." He stalked out.

Thea sent a prayer of thanks heavenward, then turned to Roth. He held himself still, controlled, but she had no doubt he could have pounced on Westerbrook at the least provocation. Yet, he had had a great deal of provocation and held his temper, which was more than she could say for herself at the moment. Her hands were still shaking from the viscount's tirade.

But if Roth could endure it all with such composure, so could she.

"Thank you, sir, for your gallant intervention," she said.

He inclined his head. "It was my pleasure. I hope you will not have to pay the price for my insolence."

Thea waved a hand. "Hardly insolence. I'd call it a truth long overdue. Still, I doubt he listened. He never does."

"If you will excuse me, I should see to your sons."

Disappointment tapped her shoulder. She ignored it. "Of course. I will see you all at dinner."

Her traitorous gaze followed him out the door.

Well! That was entirely enough of that. She'd heard of dastardly masters who made advances on the maids. She certainly wasn't going to treat her sons' tutor that way.

Though she had to own, she was looking forward to tomorrow and the wedding, and it had nothing to do with the ride in between, alone with him.

"How would you like your hair, milady?" Martin asked as Thea sat at the dressing table the next morning. Her maid idly twisted the brush in her capable hands as if she knew the answer already.

"A few curls around my face, I think," Thea said. "And I will forego the veil today. It is a wedding after all."

Martin brightened, and she set to work with a will.

She was equally delighted to hear that she would be accompanying her mistress. Thea had realized in the night that, tutor or no, it was inappropriate for her to be in an enclosed carriage with Roth for the hour it would take to reach or return from Hewett House, where the wedding was being held. He must have had a similar concern, for when he met her in the entry hall, he was dressed in a heavy, multi-caped greatcoat and wool gloves.

"I will ride with the coachman," he said.

Once again, disappointment nudged. "Don't be ridiculous. How will it look if you arrive windblown and soaked for your friend's wedding?"

As if to prove the hazard, rain began to splatter against the windows looking out on the courtyard.

Roth glanced at Martin, who was waiting by the door in her own wool cloak, then nodded. "Very well."

Victory warming her, Thea allowed him to escort her out and hand her up.

He sat across from her with Martin, who scooted over until she was pressed against the padded side of the carriage.

"I will not bite," Roth told her.

She colored, but lifted her chin. "I did not think that you would, sir. Some of us just like a little more space than others."

He faced forward and crossed his arms over his chest.

Taking up fully two-thirds of the seat.

Thea hid a smile and patted the spot beside her. "There's plenty of room, Martin. Please join me."

Her maid slipped across with a grateful smile just as the coach started out.

They came down off the hill and turned east out of the village to follow the winding path of the River Wey. The venerable stream was braided and branched as it crossed the fields. It must have been flowing since before her family built the castle.

"Dark day for a wedding," she commented as they clattered over the graceful stone bridge that arched the river. Charcoal-colored clouds spit rain from swollen bottoms.

"It is a dark time of year to wed," Roth allowed, settling his greatcoat around him. "But as Tanner and Miss Hewett wish to travel in the new year, there is no better time."

They turned onto the River Road and navigated the curve that would take them past the Thames and the entrance to Rose Hill, Lady Belfort's estate. She caught him leaning forward, as if to catch a better view.

"Did you enjoy your time at Rose Hill?" she asked.

"It is a fine estate," he allowed. "And I will always be thankful for Lady Belfort's patronage."

He hadn't answered the question directly, but she thought she understood. He had been a guest at Rose Hill. It hadn't been home.

When was the last time he'd had a home?

"Do you miss Batavaria?" she asked as they approached Weyton and Martin's head dropped onto Thea's shoulder. To the left, Thea caught a glimpse of the Duke of Wey's home on his island in the Thames. It wasn't a castle, though the locals called it such. It was simply a large house surrounded by a wall. Then again, some might say the same of her home.

"Only on occasion," he said. He did not elaborate.

She chuckled. "This is not an inquisition, Mr. Roth. I am merely trying to make conversation to pass the time."

He inclined his head. "Forgive me. It has been a long time since I was in Batavaria, more than ten years, and I fought at its borders for several years before I joined the guard. I no longer long for a glimpse of its mountains."

He glanced out the window. "Most days. It may be different for the others who stayed in England."

The carriage turned right toward Weybridge, and she knew they were getting closer.

"Mr. Tanner, the groom, was one of those who stayed, I understand," she said. "I believe I heard that he and Miss Hewett met while he was her bodyguard."

"He met her at the Duchess of Wey's house party last summer," he corrected. "They met again at the Weyton assembly earlier in the autumn. Then he became her bodyguard."

"Ah," she said, though the whole affair still sounded odd to her. "A unique courtship."

He regarded her. "Is not every courtship unique?"

"Perhaps so," she allowed with a smile. "Though most of the women who came out with me went through the same process: balls, soirees, visits to the theatre and opera, drives in Hyde Park. In the end, we each married the gentleman our parents preferred."

"I had heard it was so for much of the aristocracy," he said. "But both Prince Otto Leopold and his twin brother, Count Montalban, married women they admired above all others."

"Ah, yes, the lovely daughters of the Duke of Wey," she agreed. "You must remember, sir, that neither Lady Larissa nor Lady Calantha stand to inherit the title. That is for their brother, Lord Thalston."

"And you, in line to inherit your father's title, had to choose more carefully."

Her father would not have liked her having this conversation with a member of her staff, but he wasn't here. She was Alldene now.

"Very carefully," she confirmed. "My husband, Thomas, was the grandson of a viscount; he understood our manner of life. We grew fond of each other."

"A good outcome, then," he said.

She nodded, but she wasn't sure why something inside her protested.

It was the same when they arrived at Hewett House. Everything was lovely, but some part of her struggled. The solid block of the manor had flowered wreaths on every window and more crowded the withdrawing room where the ceremony would be held. Mr. Hewett must have raided every greenhouse for miles to find them. Still, she preferred her castle. She would have had a hard time accustoming herself to the endless views across the fields. It was too open, too exposed.

So was the love on Julia Hewett's face as the charming redhead took her beloved's hand and vowed to love, honor, and obey for as long as they lived.

Had she and Thomas ever looked at each other that way? They had been friends. They had worked together for the good of the estate and their children. They had both understood that duty must come first.

At the moment, she would have gladly shrugged off duty for one moment of such admiration, such joy.

Unbidden, her gaze sought Roth's. Across the aisle from her, he sat, face immobile. Was he pleased for his friend? Envious that he had yet to find a lady to stand beside him? Bored with the entire affair?

That disquiet poked at her again, urging her to go to his side. What had she said about duty? It would not allow such an acquaintance with her sons' tutor.

No matter how much she might wish it.

CHAPTER SEVEN

IF ONLY JULIAN were here.

Meredith, Lady Belfort, nearly sighed aloud at the refrain that had been haunting her for months, ever since her husband had set off for the Continent as part of the delegation going to ratify the agreement among England, Batavaria, and Württemberg. Julian had been the chief architect of the Batavarian Doctrine; it only made sense for him to see it to conclusion. But, oh, how she missed her husband!

He had been one to appreciate Julia's mad starts, and she thought he would enjoy seeing the energetic redhead marry Kristoff Tanner. Watching them gaze at each other, eyes shining, she could only remember her own wedding and all the wonderful years since.

Fortune wiggled in her arms, head tilted to let Meredith know of her displeasure.

"A few moments more," Meredith whispered to her pet. She was always leery of bringing Fortune to crowded locations. The cat abhorred her jeweled collar and lead and was forever rubbing against something to try to dislodge them. But Julia and Tanner had specifically requested her presence at their wedding. After all, she had been the one to match them.

As the bride and groom turned to be recognized by their guests, who rose to applaud them, Meredith's gaze moved to the other side of the impromptu aisle and her friend, Thea. How nice to see her remove that black veil and to see her smile. It seemed some of her worries had been resolved.

Yet, why was Roth about as far away from her as he could get?

"Trouble, my love," she murmured to Fortune.

Fortune's wiggles multiplied.

Meredith glanced around again as the happy couple started down the aisle. The doors to the entry hall were closed. Fortune would not be able to escape the house. Nearly everyone in attendance knew her. Surely it would be safe to let her free.

Meredith bent and set her pet on the thick carpet. "Do what you do best," she murmured as she released the lead from the collar.

"Our sixth wedding since arriving in England," Adrian Keller commented. He had joined Roth at the side of the withdrawing room as the guests took turns congratulating the bride and groom before the wedding breakfast to be held in the dining room next door.

Roth glanced at his friend. Keller was the youngest of the guards. His blond hair and guileless blue eyes often made their enemies underestimate him. Roth knew better. Keller was a force to be reckoned with.

"Which did you like best?" Keller asked. "The prince's wedding to Lady Larissa was grand."

Their prince had been married in an elaborate event in Westminster Cathedral.

"I prefer the ceremony in Lady Belfort's withdrawing room when Huber married Abigail Winchester," Roth countered. Their fellow guardsman had wed their patroness's companion earlier this year. The two had taken positions with the Marquess of Kendall to the south.

"When I marry Elspeth in January, you will be the last bachelor among us. Unless there is a lady I have not met?" Keller's golden brows went up in query.

"No," Roth said, crossing his arms over his chest. "Who would marry me? Fathers do not want a son-in-law who has been in prison, even one pardoned by the king."

Keller nudged him. "But here in England, few know about that. And the English are quite enamored with the concept of an Imperial Guard." He aimed his smile across the room, where his bride-to-be stood with her family, who were terrors in the area. Miss Hewett had agreed to invite the dreaded Bee family for Keller's sake.

"Perhaps," Roth said, but once more his gaze veered toward Lady Alldene.

She was standing across the room, up against the crimson-draped windows. Had she been an Imperial Guard, he would have thought her on duty, so clear was her face and so calm her demeanor as she scanned the space.

Even as he watched her watching the room, he spotted a sleek grey form at her feet. "Who let Fortune free?"

Keller followed his gaze, then glanced about. "Lady Belfort is with Elspeth."

And her overbearing mother was blocking any retreat. The leash that should be attached to Fortune's collar dangled from their patroness's wrist. Did she know her pet had escaped?

Just then, Garrison, the Hewett butler, opened the doors to the entry hall for those guests who would not be attending the breakfast. Fortune darted toward freedom.

Roth darted toward Fortune.

So did Lady Alldene, for he nearly collided with her within inches of the door. Just as when they had played the game at the castle, their gazes brushed.

And held, as time slipped away to the beat of his heart.

"Now, then, what are you up to, my sweet?"

Lady Belfort bent to capture her pet even as Roth hastily stepped back from Lady Alldene.

His employer.

From his former patroness's arms, Fortune regarded him archly.

"I'm glad you caught her before any harm came to her," Lady Alldene said. Odd that her voice sounded breathless, but he had heard some ladies had trouble moving quickly in the gowns they must wear.

"She certainly knows her own mind," Lady Belfort said with a fond look at her pet. She glanced up at the countess. "I believe Julia and Tanner are free, if you wanted a word."

"Of course." Lady Alldene swept off, as if Roth were no more than a painting on the wall.

"I heard that sigh," Lady Belfort said in her absence, one hand stroking Fortune's fur.

"I did not sigh," Roth replied. "It was a breath of relief that Fortune is safe."

The cat blinked at him. He had withstood the jeers of his fellow prisoners, teases from some of the Imperial Guards. Why did that look have him squirming? He adjusted his cravat.

"Very kind of you to be concerned," Lady Belfort said. "And how goes the new position? More satisfying than the first, I hope."

"Much more satisfying," he said, but he had to force himself to keep his gaze on her instead of Lady Alldene.

"Wonderful. I can tell you're having an impact."

Roth frowned. "Have you spoken with the countess?"

"No," she replied with a pleasant smile. "But I see Thea has removed her veil and curled her hair. You have clearly removed a burden from her so that she feels more comfortable putting off mourning a little."

He frowned, and this time he could not stop his gaze from going to the countess. She was standing with

Tanner and Julia, and her face was open, relaxed, free of the tension he'd seen so often.

"You think I had that effect on her?" he asked.

"Time will tell," Lady Belfort said, and her smile was as wise as her pet's.

It had been a lovely wedding. Everyone had been congenial, the food at the breakfast afterward had been excellent, and Thea had had a better time than she'd expected.

So, why did she keep remembering the look on Roth's face as they'd run into each other? It had been only a moment. A moment of strength, of the scent of bay rum cologne, of eyes like silver meeting hers. That flicker of awareness, of something more.

No, nothing more. Nothing more could come of it. He was her employee, the tutor of her sons. She was a countess with tenants and lands to administer. She hadn't protested when he'd insisted on riding with the coachman on the way home.

So, the next few days, she threw herself into her work, calling Shaw down to sit with her on one occasion. His head was level with her shoulder as he took the seat next to hers at the desk, and she tried not to sigh with this further evidence that he was growing up too fast.

"I have been informed that our herd is dwindling," she explained. "Age, infirmity, and accident can decrease the number. There is some concern about the heifers. Do you know what heifer means?"

He stopped himself in the middle of rolling his eyes and cleared his throat instead. "Yes, Mother. It is a spinster cow."

Thea nearly laughed aloud but managed to keep her tone and smile level. "A female cow that has yet to bear a calf, yes. They can be the future of the herd, if we do not slaughter them for food. How would we go about increasing their number?"

He frowned. "Perhaps we could keep more alive than usual?"

"An excellent suggestion," she said. "Let us write such an instruction to the home farm."

She also showed Shaw how to send orders to their agents in London to purchase more stock. She had decided on northern manufacturing, particularly textiles. Everyone needed socks, after all. And she explained why she was advising their bankers to transfer funds between accounts so that they would have ample money for improvements in Surrey and in Scotland.

However, she spared Shaw the meeting with Mr. Vernon, her land steward. Those meetings had become one of her more difficult tasks since Thomas had died. Vernon attended her weekly in the library, while Martin kept her company and Thea kept the door open. He was an angular fellow with cheekbones as sharp as his opinions and a beard that seemed to bristle with indignation. And sometimes she thought he delighted in bringing her complaints.

"The moat's backed up," he announced that day, shoving a drawing toward her as if to prove as much.

Was she supposed to understand the inner workings of the moat now? From her father's tutelage, she knew the water bubbled up from springs to the west of the castle and flowed out the opposite side to run down the hill in a cascade, wind through the fields, and eventually empty into the Bourne. Perhaps she should go out and inspect the moat, look for issues. Or perhaps she should task their groundskeeper.

You hired a man you respected.

Roth's words sounded in her mind. Her father had hired Vernon for this role. He'd been in the position for at least fifteen years now. Surely he had some idea of what to do.

Thea leaned back in her chair. "What are your recommendations, Mr. Vernon?"

He blinked, then a smile slowly broadened his cheeks. "I'd remove the reedmace encroaching on the southern corner and add more rocks about the spring opening to prevent silt from clogging it."

She rather liked the reedmace, for it provided a home for birds, but she could see the wisdom in keeping it out of the moat proper. "Do you have the resources to make that happen?"

"I do," he said.

"Then please do so."

Their entire discussion, which generally lasted several hours, took no more than a quarter hour, and her steward left with a spring in his step.

Well!

The meeting with Mrs. Willoughby, her housekeeper, went much the same way.

"You are highly experienced, Mrs. Willoughby," Thea told her when they met in the library. "Instead of me inquiring as to the availability of produce and meat and then laying out menus for both the family and the staff, perhaps you could develop menus for my approval. Be sure they include something that will appeal to the children. I will let you know if I am expecting any deviation from our normal routine."

Her housekeeper grinned from ear to ear. "Happy to help, your ladyship. I'll have next week's menus to you this very afternoon."

By two, she had finished most of her tasks for the week. She checked the list again, then shook her head. How delightful. Whatever was she to do with herself?

She might read a book. She had never started that latest Waverly novel of Scottish **derring-do**. Or go for a ride if it wasn't too cold. She could even look through her wardrobe, see what might be suitable when it was time to put off mourning.

Instead, she found herself climbing the stairs for the schoolroom. She told herself that it was only natural she would want to spend time with her children. It had nothing to do with the boys' tutor.

But the schoolroom was empty, and Nurse Waters was sitting alone in the rocking chair in the nursery.

"Where are the children?" Thea asked her.

She sniffed. "The boys are off to the gentlemen's salon to practice with swords. Lady Audra insisted on watching. I thought that man would refuse her, but he didn't." She took a jab at the sock she was darning with her needle. "He has no concept of how a lady should behave."

"I'll check on them," Thea promised. "Audra has a great deal of energy. Perhaps you can suggest ways she might employ it."

She sniffed again. "Young ladies are better taught to curb their energy."

Thea left without responding. It very much looked as if she would have to find a governess for Audra sooner than planned. Nurse Waters' expectations mirrored those of Thea's father, but she could not appreciate them. She had had to channel all her energy into learning to be an earl, but her daughter did not have that responsibility. Surely there was some middle ground between sedate pastimes and militant ones!

She had never understood why Thomas had decided to turn the inner hall of the castle, where the original earl and his men had met to eat and drink and decide weighty matters, into the gentlemen's salon, where he and his friends and male cousins met to pummel each other in various ways. Her mother had used the space for a ballroom on occasion. By design, the room was well secluded and well protected, to the point that only a few narrow windows on the paneled walls let in light and air, and the stone hearth was large enough to roast an ox.

The chairs on which the earl and his lady had once sat still rested against one wall. She had always thought they resembled thrones with their tall, heavy, carved backs, thick arms, and seats softened by scarlet velvet cushions. The entire affair dwarfed her daughter, who was seated on one, feet swinging under her skirts.

But Thomas had otherwise done his best to make the space look like a gentlemen's salon. The trestle tables and benches had been replaced by racks along the walls bearing practice swords, strips of cotton for wrapping fists, puffy gloves for boxing, and targets for the bows and arrows. With lamps blazing along the walls, Shaw and James faced each other across the wood floor, practice swords at the ready. The dulled blades looked impossibly long for either of them, though Shaw held his the steadiest.

"Good," Roth was saying from the side of the room. "Now, Master James, advance, and Lord Shaw, defend."

James thrust at his brother, and Shaw knocked it aside easily. Audra clapped. Then he slashed the blade at James, hitting him squarely across the chest.

"You're dead," Shaw announced as James stumbled back.

"That's cheating!" Audra cried even as Thea started forward.

Roth beat her to it, positioning himself between them, gaze on her youngest. "Are you all right, Master James?"

James rubbed at his chest with his free hand, glowering around Roth at his brother. "Never better."

Shaw snorted.

Roth rounded on him. "Did I tell you to attack?" he demanded.

Shaw paled. "No, but I clearly had the advantage."

"Because your brother expected you to behave as a

gentleman," Roth told him. "I told you to defend. What would your general do if one of his soldiers disobeyed an order?"

Shaw lowered the blade. "Send him to a court-martial. Father said you must have discipline in the ranks, or all is lost."

Thea bit her lip to keep from commenting. Discipline and Thomas had seemed only briefly acquainted.

"And should a general ever take advantage of one of his men?" Roth pressed.

Shaw hung his head. "No. The others will not follow him." He glanced around Roth. "Sorry, James. It won't happen again. You can strike me, if you like."

James rubbed at his chest again. "I'd rather earn that strike, if you don't mind."

Shaw smiled, raising his sword. "I won't make it easy."

With a nod, Roth stepped back.

Thea closed her eyes a moment, relief and pride warring. Then she went to join her daughter. Her movement must have finally alerted them to her presence, because James waved, Shaw nodded with respect and no doubt a little concern, and Roth clapped his fist to his chest in salute.

"Can't I please fight too, Mother?" Audra begged as Thea sat on the chair standing next to hers. "I want to poke at Shaw."

Shaw started laughing even as he raised his blade again. "Girls can't fence, Audra."

Tears pooled in her daughter's eyes, eyes so like her father's, as she gazed at Thea. "Girls don't get to have any fun."

"Girls have a great deal of fun," Thea corrected her. "They dance the night away at balls, they play music with their friends to the acclaim of their families. They are sought after, admired. Sometimes even fought over."

The words only seemed to frustrate her daughter more. "But they don't get to fight back."

She felt the injustice of it as well. Odd. She had been trained to lead men, but she had never been taught to fight beside them. Would it truly be so scandalous?

"I suppose there's no reason why a girl cannot learn to fence," she reasoned, "if that's truly what you want, Audra."

Gaze now shining, her daughter nodded eagerly.

The others were all watching them.

"Really?" James asked.

"Do you fence, Mother?" Shaw asked. She could hear the challenge in his words.

That, at least, she had been trained to battle. "No," she admitted, "but if you're learning, I'm certain I could as well."

James recoiled. "Who would teach a girl to fence?"

"The same person who teaches the gentlemen, I imagine," Thea said, avoiding Roth's gaze.

"Who would practice with you?" James persisted, and this time he sounded a little worried.

"As we are of different heights," Thea said, "I'm not sure it would be wise for me to face off with either of you."

James smiled. Shaw nodded as if satisfied.

But she was not so ready to concede defeat. There was an answer, and, when she glanced his way, she found he was still watching her as if he expected what she was going to say.

"So," Thea continued, "what do you say, Mr. Roth? Would you fence with me?"

CHAPTER EIGHT

ANOTHER CHALLENGE? DID she still doubt him? But no, he could only call the light in her eyes excitement. Something kindled in his blood as well.

The boys were watching him. Shaw was trying to hide it by glancing away and then back even as he rested the tip of his blunted sword on the floor. James was shuffling his feet and biting his lower lip as he looked to his mother, as if very much fearing she was about to be slashed. Roth would never have hurt her for the world.

Them either. The last few days they had spent the late afternoons searching for the children's treasure. He'd chosen a time close enough to dinner that the staff would be busy elsewhere, so no one remarked on their movements. They had only passed Hartshorn, the footman, twice, and on both occasions he had not questioned them, though Roth felt his curious gaze following their movements.

They had found no treasure, ghosts, or monsters. He had only been forced to rush the children back upstairs once to scrub their hands and brush down their clothes before dinner after they'd climbed through the dungeons to no avail.

"We're never going to find it," James had lamented last night before Roth had taken them all down to the dining room.

"Yes, we will," Audra had insisted, but even her enthusiasm had dampened.

"Patience is often rewarded," Roth had assured them. "We've only covered a quarter of the castle. Lord Shaw, how much does that mean we have left?"

"Three-quarters," the boy had declared.

"Seventy-five percent," James had agreed with a sigh.

Perhaps a fencing demonstration would give them something else to occupy their minds.

"Very well, your ladyship," Roth said with a bow. "Master James, would you offer your sword to your mother, hilt first? Lord Shaw, I will borrow yours."

James carefully twisted his sword to hand it to his mother, who accepted it with a smile.

Shaw offered his blade to Roth.

"She favors her left hand," he whispered before backing away.

Interesting. Did the lad think Thea could best him? Or was he warning Roth to go easy on her?

And when had he started thinking of her as Thea?

She swished the blade through the air as he took up a position opposite her.

"It's heavier than I expected," she mused.

"Hold it up, Mother," James advised. "It's easier that way."

Immediately she raised the tip. "Ah, yes. I see. Thank you, James."

He colored.

"Stand with one foot forward, the other back," Shaw advised as if not to be outdone. "And turn your body a little so you offer a smaller target."

At least they'd listened to Roth's instruction. He watched as Thea did likewise.

"Five minutes," he said. "No need to keep score."

"Why, Mr. Roth," she said, "where's the fun in that? First one to score two points wins."

One minute then. Already, her arm looked as if it were trembling from holding the blade.

She saluted him with it, then brought it up before her. "Lay on, sir!"

She must have seen a match or two to use the term, or perhaps she'd read it in one of the histories of the castle. It was a call used by knights and courtiers. He was neither, but nothing said he could not play the gentleman.

Roth tapped his blade against hers. She pushed back. Her husband must have had some skills to own these fine practice swords. He circled to the right, and she matched him.

"Don't let him get under your guard, Mother," Shaw warned.

"Smack him!" Audra cried.

Thea watched him as he moved the other direction. Her gaze was razor sharp, her chest rising and falling as she breathed. No, she wasn't having an easy time of it.

He lunged.

She parried and scrambled out of reach.

"No, Mother," Shaw scolded. "Stand up to him."

"It's your turn to hit him," Audra put in.

"There aren't turns in this type of fight, Audra," Thea said. Before he could gauge her next move, she lunged.

Roth parried easily, then drove his blade home, the flat of the saber pressing against the black fabric.

She stepped back, shrugging one shoulder.

"One point to Mr. Roth," James said.

Her eyes narrowed. Before he could resume his stance, she rushed at him. He twisted away, but not before he felt the blade brush his arm.

"And one point for Mother!" Audra caroled, hopping out of her chair.

They faced off against each other again. Her blade was not quite as high as it had been. It wouldn't be difficult to score his second point. Some might have assumed he would lose on purpose. Besting your employer was never wise. But he didn't think she would want him to pretend to be less than he was.

He brought the blade down, and she managed to push it away before it struck. He pressed his advantage, and their blades ran along each other to clang against the hilts. For a moment, they were face to face, body to body, their blades the only things between them. And, for a moment, he was lost in the depths of her eyes.

She pulled back and brought her sword against his arm.

"Two points!" James cried.

"Mother wins, Mother wins," Audra sang, dancing around the edge of the practice floor.

A slow smile curved Thea's lips, and her eyes sparkled like diamonds as she dropped her arm. She had defeated him, something rare enough among the Imperial Guards that it would have been marked by shouting and applauding.

But he found he couldn't mind in the least.

Why hadn't Thomas ever allowed her to practice with him? It was like a dance, only faster, closer. In fact, it was absolutely exhilarating. She felt like skipping about with Audra.

Some men might have been annoyed to have been bested, particularly by a woman who had just picked up the blade, but Roth was smiling as if he couldn't have been prouder.

He lowered his blade, inclined his head, and pressed a fist to his chest. "I yield to my victor."

"The honor was mine, sir," she said, using her free hand to spread one side of her skirts in a curtsey. She would not allow him to see how much her arm shook from the effort. "James, come take your sword."

Her youngest son scurried forward, eyes wide. At least she'd gone up a notch in his estimation. Shaw's too, she thought, by the way her oldest was regarding her.

"Let me try, Mother," Audra said, coming to wrap her arms around Thea's skirts. "Please?"

Such an earnest little face. Thea brushed a wisp of hair off the girl's forehead. "No, Audra, you will wait."

Audra's face started puckering.

"Not because you're a girl," Thea assured her, "but because those swords are long and heavy. I was right in my previous assessment. Fencing isn't safe for you right now. When you reach this high," she put her hand under her bosom, "you may learn, if you still want to, of course."

Audra released her and nodded. "I will. Thank you, Mother."

"We are finished today, in any event," Roth said. He handed his blade to Shaw. "See that these are put away."

She waited for her oldest son to inform his tutor he was beneath such things, but Shaw beckoned to James with his free hand, and the two went to carry the blades over to a rack against the far wall.

"You are a magician, sir," she murmured to Roth. "I have seldom seen my sons obey so readily."

Audra must have heard her, for she swished her skirts. "They know we have something better to do."

"Better than fencing?" Thea teased. "What could that possibly be?"

"Sums," Shaw said with a warning look to his sister. "So we'd better get to it."

He and James marched manfully out the door, Audra skipping behind.

"Sums?" Thea asked with a look to Roth.

Pink had stained his cheeks, but perhaps it was from the exertion. "James is exceptionally good at arithmetic. Shaw feels the need to catch up and best him. If you'll excuse me."

He left faster than if she'd been chasing him with a blade.

"They are certainly determined in their quest," she told Martin when she'd asked her maid's assistance in changing her chemise. Even after that short fight, she could feel perspiration dribbling down her back.

"Just being boys, I warrant," Martin said, working the tapes at the side of Thea's gown.

About time, too. Shaw would one day have to take over the title and all the duties that went with it, but at least, for now, he could just be a boy.

Even if she had to fight Westerbrook to keep it that way.

She had hoped his visit earlier in the week had been sufficient to discharge his obligations to her sons, so she was surprised when Felden announced him on Saturday. She had actually had a moment to curl up in the library with her Scotch novel and was just at the point where the hero confronted the villain when she heard Felden clear his throat.

"Forgive the interruption, your ladyship," he said when she looked at him askance. "Lord Westerbrook is here to see you."

All enjoyment fled. " Show him to the withdrawing room, Felden," she said, casting her story one more glance before setting it aside and rising.

Thomas's cousin had been standing by the hearth, but the moment she entered the room, he came toward her, hands out. "Thea, dear!"

"Westerbrook," she replied, neatly sidestepping him to go sit on the sofa. Too late she realized he had enough room to sit beside her and was thankful when he didn't sit at all. Instead, he made a point of strolling about the room as if admiring her furnishings and decor.

"And where are my charming wards?" he asked, pausing

to gaze at a landscape painting of a farm dale. "Deep in a battle with their lead soldiers, no doubt."

"Likely studying," Thea replied. "That is why you suggested I find a better tutor for them, after all."

She waited for him to renew his demands that she discharge Roth. Might as well get it over with, after all. Perhaps he would leave sooner.

He merely nodded. "Quite right, though a break from one's studies on occasion is always wise. It keeps the mind fresh." He turned and looked to her butler, who was standing along one wall. "Bring the lads down, Felden."

He would order her staff in her own house? Thea stiffened. Felden drew himself up as well and looked to her for confirmation. She bit back a retort and nodded, and her butler stepped out.

Westerbrook turned to her, face softening. "I have begun to realize that I have been too hard on you, Thea. It must have been difficult for you, alone here without Thomas. How matters must weigh on you."

Now he noticed? A shame he hadn't figured it out while he was making the year even more difficult. At least the challenges had seemed less of late, as if she were a Thoroughbred hitting her stride. "I have managed."

"You have indeed. Courageously." He made another circuit of the room, going so far as to pick up an alabaster box, examine it, and set it down. "You pass out of mourning in a few weeks, if I recall."

Was that judgment? "Life goes on, my lord. I'm sure Thomas would wish to put off mourning had our positions been reversed."

"No doubt, no doubt." He sucked his teeth a moment before coming to join her on the sofa at last.

"You must know you can lean on me if your troubles become too much," he said, edging closer.

Never. Under any circumstance. "You are too kind," she said, leaning away from him. "But we will prevail."

"Excellent attitude," he commended her with a smile. "That is one of the things that I have always admired about you, Thea. You are absolutely unflappable."

If he knew the many times she had cried herself to sleep since Thomas's passing, he would not praise her so. In fact, she wasn't entirely sure why he was praising her at all, especially after arguing with her over every little matter. She was just thankful the boys came in then.

And even more relieved to see Roth with them. "There are my wards!" Westerbrook spread his arms as if he would hug them both. "Come make your bows, my boys, and tell me all about how you're getting on."

Shaw and James exchanged glances, but they came forward and offered him very credible bows. She caught Roth's eye, where he had joined Felden along the wall, and knew he was pleased with their performance as well.

"Lord Westerbrook," Shaw said, straightening. "How have you been?"

"I am well, thank you for asking," Westerbrook said. "And you?"

"Tolerable," Shaw said.
Thea bit back a smile. "Lord Westerbrook wanted to assure himself of your health and well-being," she explained. "As your guardian, that is his obligation."

James frowned, but Westerbrook waved a hand. "Never an obligation, but a privilege, boys. Tell me, do either of you play the piano?"

"We both do," Shaw said, and now he was frowning too. "You have heard us practice before."

"Ah, of course. Silly of me to forget. Favor us with your most recent piece. Whatever your tutor taught you."

So, that was his game. He was still trying to show Roth up. Against the wall, her sons' valiant tutor had stiffened as well, though his face betrayed none of his emotions.

Thea opened her mouth to protest the imposition, but Shaw spoke first.

"I'd be delighted." He strolled to the pianoforte, perched on the bench, and set his fingers to the ivory keys.

She couldn't help it. She glanced at Roth again. He met her gaze and shrugged.

She couldn't imagine what her son intended to play, for he had no music in front of him, and he hadn't practiced since Thomas had passed to her knowledge. Yet Shaw launched into a military air with passion. She didn't recognize it, but she was fairly certain no composer had put those notes together. James grimaced a few times at the discordant sounds. She steeled herself for Westerbrook's criticism.

"Very nice," he said as the last note faded. "You have obviously been practicing."

Thea blinked but kept her mouth shut as Shaw rose to return to her side.

Westerbrook turned to her younger son. "And James, I believe you sing?"

James looked as if he were choking as his panicked gaze swept from Thea to Roth.

"He has complained of a sore throat," Roth put in. "I would not advise straining it with a song."

Bless him! James nodded rapidly and attempted to look regretful.

"Of course," Westerbrook crooned. "I would never want to see the least harm come to my boys. Now, I've taken entirely too much of your time. Come shake my hand like gentlemen, and I will have your tutor return you to your studies."

Shaw took his turn, then James in shaking Westerbrook's hand. Roth looked to Thea, and it took everything in her to nod and allow him to leave the room with them.

Felden remained behind, gaze on Lord Westerbrook as if ready for the least infraction.

"You are blessed with two wonderful children," Westerbrook said with a sigh in the boys' absence.

"I am blessed with *three* wonderful children," she corrected him. "Perhaps you will be able to say the same one day."

He pressed a hand to his paisley waistcoat. "Oh, if only that were true. My heart has been broken so many times. It is difficult to find a lady who understands me as you do, Thea."

Her smile was frozen to her face. "Thank you for calling, my lord."

At least he took the hint. He rose and bent over her hand. She tried not to cringe as his lips brushed her knuckles. "Always a pleasure, dear Thea."

If he purred her name one more time she would be very tempted to take one of the practice swords to his hide. Even Felden looked pleased to be escorting him out.

Thea leaned back on the sofa with a shake of her head. Why this sudden interest in the boys? Why this sudden interest in *her*? He gained nothing by flattery.

What was he up to?

"I wish he wouldn't show up whenever he likes," Shaw groused as Roth led them back to the schoolroom. "We have better things to do."

He would rather have stayed. Lord Westerbrook had been in an odd mood. Roth didn't like leaving Thea alone with him. But he had been dismissed, and a soldier did not question his commanding officer.

"You do not care for your father's friend?" Roth asked as he and the boys settled around the worktable in the schoolroom.

"He was never Father's friend," Shaw countered hotly.

"He is Father's cousin," James explained to Roth. "You

cannot disown family." He sounded sincerely saddened by the fact.

Shaw had a different opinion. "Yes, you can," he argued. "A father can disown a son, even if he cannot keep his heir from the title. Father could have distanced himself. But Lord Westerbrook bullied him, just as he tries to bully Mother."

James sighed. "I can't abide bullies." He glanced at Shaw, then quickly away.

"No gentleman should abide a bully," Roth said. "Now, let us attend to lessons. You will be expected to understand your family's lineage. We will sketch it."

It was an illuminating exercise, for him more than the boys, he thought. The House of Alldene had its roots deep in history, before the Normans had conquered England. Its connections reached into a number of titled families, the most recent the Westerbrook viscountcy.

Roth frowned down at Shaw's carefully aligned drawing. "Then you are Lord Westerbrook's heir as well as your mother's."

"His heir presumptive," Shaw pointed out. "Only until he marries and has a son of his own."

James made a face. "Who would marry him?"

Roth chose not to comment. At least he knew why Thea insisted on allowing the villain access to her home. She had made no secret of her antipathy for the fellow, but his guardianship and family connection to her husband put her in the position of having to receive him.

But was it only duty that returned the fellow to her side so often?

CHAPTER NINE

THE THOUGHT THAT Lord Westerbrook might be pursuing Thea rolled around in Roth's mind as he lay on his bed that night. The room might be perfectly situated to keep an eye on his charges, but it had no window and no hearth, and it only grew colder as the night lengthened. All too conducive to brooding.

She saw the viscount as her enemy, but at least Westerbrook was of her own class. Given her responsibilities, she would have few opportunities to interact with others like him, particularly now that winter had arrived. And it sounded as if she would not be out of mourning until the new year. Surely she would not consider him as a suitor. The very thought chilled his blood more than the night air.

He pulled the covers closer, but the feeling didn't abate. He needed to regain control of himself. He was a tutor, nothing more. She was not the woman for him. If he wanted a wife, he must look elsewhere than a countess.

Even if he began to think that no other woman could match her.

Sunday, he sat in the church gallery again, gazing down at the children and Thea and trying not to imagine what it would be like to worship at their sides. Nurse Waters was in the pew behind them. Perhaps he would be as welcome, but a distance would yawn between them nonetheless. He was not their equal. Someday, his charges would head for school, and he would be out of a job.

As the day was clear, he walked back to the castle with Felden and the others. It was his half day off, but he had promised Shaw and James he would help them search the entry hall. With many of the staff off duty as well, it was the perfect time, even if he had to send Hartshorn away on some errand, to which he went with a mutter and a dark glance back. They found nothing before it was time for tea and games with Thea.

This week she played the pianoforte for the children, fingers graceful on the keys, and they sang songs together. Most Roth didn't know, but he liked listening and watching Thea glow.

Dinner was even better. In fact, dinner was one of the best parts of his day. They would all meet in the opulent dining room, settling at one end of the table. She would ask the children about their day, and each would tell her some fact that generally included him. Thea would meet his gaze and smile. And he would try not to smile back, especially with Nurse Waters glaring at him. He was allowed to be proud of his charges' progress. He just shouldn't be so pleased about their mother's least glance.

On Monday, he was instructing Shaw and James on rudiments of the French language when Audra bounced into the schoolroom, muslin skirts flapping about her legs. Waters trailed her. Why did the nurse always look as if she'd just sucked a lemon? She'd had more time to herself since Roth had arrived than she ever could have before. Thank goodness Audra seemed to take no notice as she came up to Roth, where he stood at the end of the worktable, and slipped her hand into his.

"I want to learn to box," she announced.

Shaw and James eagerly set aside their slates.

Waters sighed as she joined them. "I tried to dissuade her, but she will not listen. Tell her this is foolishness, Mr.

Roth. A young lady has no need to go about striking people." She scowled at Audra.

"We all would like the ability to defend ourselves and those we love," Roth replied. He crouched to put himself on Audra's level. The little girl's dark eyes were bright with anticipation. "You have many to defend you, Lady Audra. Why do you want to learn to box?"

She glanced at Shaw. "I don't like bullies."

Shaw busied himself with his slate again, as if conjugating French verbs had suddenly taken on a new fascination.

"Neither do I," James said with a nod of support.

Nurse Waters drew herself up. "If you are being bullied, Lady Audra, you just tell me. I will see the matter stopped."

Waters might scold Shaw, but Roth doubted the boy would heed her. Even now he was mumbling under his breath as he scrawled on his slate.

"If I teach you," Roth said to Audra, "I would expect you to honor my instruction. Just because you are capable of using your fists doesn't mean you can forego using your words first."

"Some people," Audra said, gaze still latched on her oldest brother, "don't listen to words."

What had the boy done? The last few times Audra had joined them, Shaw had been more focused on searching than lording over his little sister.

"Some words," Shaw said archly, making a flourish on his slate, "are not worth listening to."

Roth rose. "I will teach you and Master James. Nurse Waters, what time would be convenient for Lady Audra's schedule?"

She huffed, and she puffed, but she finally appointed a time on Wednesday afternoon. Then she took Audra's hand and dragged her from the schoolroom. Audra waved her free hand at Roth before disappearing.

"Why is your sister intent on punishing you?" Roth asked Shaw.

James edged away from his brother on the bench as if he thought he might face the same consequences.

"I'm sure I have no idea," Shaw said, head bent over his slate. "But they don't have to like me. They only have to respect me."

"That may be true of a general and his troops," Roth allowed, bracing his hands on the table. "But it should not be true of those closest to you. I can tell your mother is very proud of you. She loves you."

Shaw sniffed, but not from his usual disdain, Roth thought. Unless he was mistaken, the boy was fighting tears.

"She loves us all," James seemed compelled to remind them.

"That is evident," Roth agreed. "James, would you see if you can find the French history book we were looking at last week? I believe it is on the far bookshelf."

The boy nodded and headed for the other side of the schoolroom. Roth went to sit beside Shaw, who hunched more tightly over his work.

"You have the makings of an exceptional earl," he told the boy. "You think through issues before acting. You are logical and decisive. Every day, you grow in wisdom."

Shaw glanced up at him. That heaviness was back on his face, as if he worried even more than James. "Father was very good at helping Mother. She doesn't ask me for help."

"I cannot know what's in your mother's mind," Roth admitted, "but I think she wants to give you the chance to enjoy your time learning. Too much work too soon can make a child bitter. I know this to be a fact."

Shaw frowned. "Did you have to work when you were young?"

"As young as Audra," he said as James returned and slipped into his place next to his brother, setting the book on the table. "In a silver mine, going places the men could not reach. They even sent me in when they feared the air was poisoned. If I passed out, they knew it wasn't safe for them."

James stared at him. "How did they get you out?"

"They had a rope tied to my ankle," he said, surprised the memory no longer stung. "They yanked me out."

Shaw crossed his arms over his chest. "Your father should have put a stop to that."

"My father was dead. My mother too. And the great-uncle who took me in owned the silver mine. So, you see, I know something about bullies." He leaned closer. "It is too easy for men like us to become one. But only you can make that decision."

Shaw nodded, then bent back over his work. So did James. Roth could only hope the older boy would heed his words, before one of his siblings felt the need to take him down a peg.

Thea kept expecting Westerbrook to come striding in, but he did not appear on Monday or Tuesday. She was just as glad. The last visit had been completely unsettling, and she could not forget the way he had kissed her hand, holding it in such a proprietary manner.

He could not be attempting to court her. He must know by now that she had little use for him. Her estate produced abundantly, her investments acceptably, but neither would be enough for him. And he would never have consented to be her consort.

Her biggest challenge at the moment, however, concerned her tenant to the east, Mr. Ufford. Water from the moat ultimately watered his fields and animals. The water had frozen before during particularly cold winters. She remembered seeing it from her bedchamber window, glassy and dark. First her father and then Thomas would tell Vernon to deal with the matter. But she had risen to find the moat iced over so thickly it sparkled in the sunlight, and Vernon had brought her no plan on how to fix it.

"I want to go ice skating," Audra said that night at dinner. "The moat is frozen. I saw it from the nursery window. May we, Mother, please?"

"The ice may be thick enough to support you, Audra," Thea told her, poking at her roast duck, "but I must find a way to thaw it if Mr. Ufford and his animals are to have water to drink."

"Your steward does not have a boat?" Roth asked, dark brows knitting.

He did not often speak at dinner, but she had found him to be good company, far better than Nurse Waters. Thea had received a great deal of pleasure glancing down the table and sharing his smile at the children's antics.

"For the river, certainly," Thea allowed. "But the ice is quite frozen. I don't see how a boat could manage it."

"My great-uncle owned a silver mine in Batavaria," he explained. "When the river used for navigation froze and we could not move the silver, he would send his men out in flat-bottomed boats, pulled by horses on the shore. His men would break up the ice around the boat with axes to make way for the larger boats carrying the silver. I would think the same process could be applied here."

She beamed at him. "An excellent suggestion, Mr. Roth. I'll advise Mr. Vernon to try that tomorrow morning. It seems your great-uncle was very wise."

"And very mean," Shaw muttered, flattening a piece of broccoli with his fork.

She frowned at him. "Do you need to apologize, young man?"

Shaw reddened and looked to Roth.

Roth shook his head. "No need. Lord Shaw understands my relationship with my great-uncle."

Shaw nodded and returned to his dinner.

She should not pry, but she was too curious to keep quiet. "Is there something I should know?"

He nodded to Carter, their head footman, who brought him more duck. "My parents died when I was younger than Audra," he told Thea as he took a second helping. "The only family left was a great-aunt and her husband. He was willing to take me in, if I could provide a service. I worked in the mine alongside the men until I was sixteen."

Shaw set down his fork and leveled his gaze on Thea. "They made him breathe poisonous air," he said, clearly incensed. "We will never treat our tenants or staff that way."

Nurse Waters huffed as if even she agreed.

"Certainly not," Thea said. "And you have reminded me of my duty, Shaw." She turned to her butler, who was standing along the wall with Carter. "Felden, fill whatever tubs are available with water and have them delivered to Hollydale Farm this evening. Tell Mr. Ufford that we will do all we can to send him more as quickly as possible."

"Of course, your ladyship." He looked to the footman, who hurried for the door to the servants' corridor.

She glanced back at the table to find Roth watching her, face noncommittal. What a difficult upbringing he'd had! But how commendable that he'd managed to rise in rank in the military to become one of his king's most trusted guards.

Still, their lives could not have been more different. Why did it feel as if they fit so well?

Why had he told her about his childhood? Given her own, she could only despise his poor upbringing. There was no castle, no loving father helping him grow into his potential. There was only privation and hardship. If not for the war with Napoleon, he might have met a sorry end.

At least he hadn't told her the most shameful part: that the tutor she was coming to appreciate had once been a thief.

So, he focused on his work on Wednesday, schooling the boys in history and natural philosophy before taking James and Audra over to the practice room for boxing lessons.

"Am I not allowed to attend?" Shaw had demanded when Roth had written him a set of mathematical problems to complete in the meantime.

"You are the oldest," Roth had said. "You have more important things you must learn." He'd pointed to the slate. "Show your mother what you can do."

With a sigh, Shaw had bent over his task.

Now Roth showed the two younger children how to protect their fists. Their father's specially made padded gloves called mufflers were far too large, but fighters had been making do for years with less. Roth had located long strips of material that would serve the purpose. The wrapping tripled the size of their fists, a fact that seemed to concern James and absolutely delighted Audra.

"My fists are as big as yours," she chortled, smacking her knuckles together as Roth began to wrap his own hands.

"For now," he said with a smile.
He had the two children face off against him on the floor.

"As we did with fencing, left foot forward, right one back," he instructed. "Again, you want to present as small a target as possible."

Immediately, James assumed the position, and Audra copied him, though she frowned down at her muslin gown, which was stretched taut to her legs.

"My skirts get in the way," she complained.

"We can do nothing about that at the moment," Roth said. "But your mother promised you wider skirts. We should ask her about them at dinner."

Audra nodded agreement.

"Now, then," Roth said, bringing up his fists. "Hold your hands so. Curl your fingers so tight water couldn't leak out and bend your thumb along the outside. Think of them as little hills and the river that runs along them."

Audra made two credible fists.

So did James, though he eyed his thumbs. "Wouldn't it be better if the thumbs were on the inside?"

"No," Roth told him. "Because a hard enough hit would injure your thumb. River on the outside. Left fist forward, right fist a little closer to your chest."

He had them raise their fists like his and practice throwing punches into the air. Jabs with their left hand, turning their bodies, followed by a strike with the force of their right as they took a step. Then he showed them how to block an opponent's blow. Sir Matthew Bateman, the former pugilist, had told him the English disdained blocking with the forearm, preferring to meet fist to fist. Prideful nonsense. If someone was attacking, you had every right to defend yourself by whatever means necessary.

Overall, he was pleased with his pupils' progress. James struggled a little with the quick movements, but Audra never wavered. He would have to watch her next time Shaw decided to criticize her.

The boy had finished his problems when Roth returned. James smirked at his brother before going to find their French book.

Roth looked over the slate.

"Excellent work," he said. "I can see I'll have to devise greater challenges."

Now Shaw smirked.

Both boys were still in fine spirits when they descended for dinner that night. Audra remembered her concern, for as soon as Thea had finished saying the blessing over the food, she piped up.

"When will I have my new skirts, Mother? These are terrible for boxing."

"Boxing?" Thea glanced at Roth. "Why, Mr. Roth, are you teaching my daughter to fight after all?"

"He is," Nurse Waters interjected, looking hopefully at their employer as if expecting her to intervene.

His neck felt hot, but he attacked his sturgeon rather than tug at his cravat. "Lady Audra requested it, and I did not see the harm. She will practice against James only. He is closer to her height."

"But at least an inch higher," James pointed out.

"And a gentleman through and through," Thea said, turning her smile on her son. "I'm sure you will not go overly hard on your sister."

James looked skeptical. "Well, if she starts it…"

"I will finish it," Roth assured them all.

"So when will I have my new skirts?" Audra persisted.

"I've been a little busy, sweetheart," Thea said. "But I hope to call the seamstress out after the new year."

Audra frowned, then brightened. "The new year? That's right! Christmas is coming!"

So it was. What would it feel like to celebrate Christmas away from his comrades for the first time in more than a decade?

And how would it feel to watch Thea and the children celebrate and know he could never truly be part of the family?

CHAPTER TEN

BETWEEN BOXING AND studies, Roth could not find time for the children to search for their treasure on Thursday or Friday. Shaw went so far as to protest as Roth was leading him and James back upstairs after dinner Saturday night. Nurse Waters had already turned for the nursery suite when Shaw caught his arm.

"We are behind schedule," he said, glancing around Roth as if to be certain his sister couldn't overhear. "We should search tonight."

James looked up and down the corridor. "Must we?"

"Yes," Shaw insisted. "It's almost Christmas. Think how much more Mother will enjoy it if she doesn't have to worry."

"But the ghost…" James started.

"There is no ghost," Roth told him. "Let me speak to your valet and explain that you will see to your own needs tonight."

He had met Monsieur Dumart shortly after taking the tutor's position. The Frenchman was only a little taller than Shaw and almost as slender. Very likely he could have been valet to a fine gentleman, but he took great pride in helping the boys dress and caring for their clothing.

"You have mischief planned, *oui*?" he asked Roth, twirling one end of his long grey mustache. "What prank tonight?"

"I do not play pranks," Roth informed him. "We are merely taking the opportunity to study later than usual."

Dumart seemed almost disappointed.

They had decided to search the chapel that night. From what Roth had seen, it was a small room, sparsely furnished, but with several low cupboards along one wall. The boys rummaged through them while he kept an eye on the corridor. James and Shaw were putting away the vestments they'd found when Roth heard it.

The sound of footsteps, moving haltingly down the dark corridor.

He glanced at James, but the boy was busy with his work and apparently hadn't noticed. Roth stepped out into the corridor and listened hard. There, heading toward the dining room.

"Stay here," he told the boys.

They exchanged glances as he started away.

It wouldn't be easy to go silently along the hardwood floor in his boots. Alldene Castle was well-maintained but old. A board creaked here, popped there. Better to confront anyway. Fists at the ready, he strode toward the sound. Ahead, he caught a flash of blue light. He quickened his steps and barreled into the dining room.

Moonlight trickled through the windows on either side of the hearth, enough to show him the room was empty. He looked under the table, seeing little in the shadows, and checked the room the servants used for preparation, but it was clear that James's phantom was gone.

"Did you catch the ghost?" the boy asked when Roth returned a few minutes later.

"No," he admitted. "But you are right, James. Someone is moving about the castle at night, and I want to know who."

He stayed close to the boys until they were safely abed, which seemed to comfort James and annoy Shaw. But he heard no other odd footsteps.

He was up before the boys on Sunday as usual and checked with Felden when he came down for a breakfast tray.

"Who monitors the castle at night?" he asked the butler, who was supervising breakfast preparations for the children and Thea.

"The footmen take it in shifts," he said.

"Do they carry a light?" Roth asked.

Felden frowned. "Yes. It is rather dark most nights. The previous earl did not like wasting candles to light all the rooms. Is there a problem, Mr. Roth?"

"I don't know," he said. "The boys and I were up later than usual and on the ground floor. I thought I heard footsteps, but I saw no one."

Felden's frown eased. "Don't listen to Master James. The castle isn't haunted."

Not by a ghost, but Roth was fairly sure someone had been about. "Tell the footmen to be watchful."

Felden took a step back, and Roth realized he'd just given his superior a direct order. He inclined his head. "Forgive me, Mr. Felden. Ordering people about is a hard habit to break."

Felden patted his shoulder. "I imagine it is."

Roth took his tray and went to prepare for services.

"And what shall we do this afternoon?" Thea asked as she, Roth, and the children were returning to the castle in the carriage later that morning. He had once more been invited to join them, both on the way down and on the way back, even though the sun had made a weak attempt to break through the grey clouds and the day was warmer than the last few.

Beside her mother, Audra raised her head. "We haven't

driven in the pony cart in ever so long. Mr. Roth could come with us."

Thea smiled down at her. "This is supposed to be Mr. Roth's time to himself. If we accompany him, we rather defeat the purpose."

Audra's face fell.

"I'd enjoy a ride." The words were out before he thought better of them. "With all of you."

"Exercise is good for you," Shaw informed his mother. "And I haven't had much time to ride lately."

"Me either," James said with a long-suffering sigh.

Thea trilled a laugh he felt to his bones. "Well, then, who am I to refuse? We will return to the castle for appropriate clothing and go for a ride."

He did not own a riding coat, but the trousers he had worn most days as an Imperial Guard would do. Topped with his greatcoat, he had every expectation of warmth and ability to move.

He wasn't sure where the stables lay, but they all returned downstairs to find three horses and a pony and cart ready for their use. Grooms assisted Shaw and James onto their mounts. Roth swung up on the black Thoroughbred by himself. Thea tucked Audra in her caped wool coat a little closer before taking up the reins on the cart. The blue of Thea's quilted pelisse brightened her eyes and softened her countenance. He wasn't sure why she was wearing it rather than her usual black, but perhaps it was one she had not dyed for mourning.

"Let's give Mr. Roth a proper tour," she told her children. She clucked to the pony, and they set out through the archway and across the drawbridge for the road down the hill.

The sun felt good against his face as they descended onto the flat. She turned right out of the village and followed the base of the hill.

Shaw, who was riding on Roth's left on a fine roan, nodded toward the fields stretching out, brown and waiting. "Those are all ours."

"Our tenant farmers'," Thea clarified. "The home farm is to the north of the castle."

"Race you to the barn!" James cried before spurring his dappled grey mount. He and Shaw took off down the road.

Roth glanced to Thea, who laughed. "They couldn't be safer here. Let them have fun."

He dropped back beside her. "It is good to hear you laugh."

Immediately she colored, but Audra cuddled closer to her. "My mother has a beautiful laugh."

"She does indeed," Roth agreed.

Thea's color only deepened. "And my daughter has a beautiful laugh as well." She fisted the reins in one hand and poked at her daughter with the other.

Audra collapsed against the padded side of the cart in a fit of giggles.

They reached the farm a short time later. Barns ran in a row, plump and sturdy, as if they were proud to be filled. There were even two greenhouses. Workers came to take the horses, and the children wandered happily among the cows, sheep, and pigs while Mr. Pennison, the head of the farm, stammered a report to Thea, hat turning in his capable hands.

"I take it you do not visit often," Roth said as they followed the children toward the barn that housed chickens.

"Mr. Vernon, my land steward, generally handles all matters with the home farm," she told him, one hand lifting her skirts out of the straw on the path. "I'd forgotten how much the children enjoy coming here. I used to love it as a girl." She nodded to a tall tree between two of the barns. "There used to be a swing there."

Roth peered closer. "There appears to still be a swing. Would you like to…"

He had meant to suggest they ask the children if they would like to take turns, but she seized his hand and tugged him over, then settled her skirts on the wide plank of the swing. She kicked at the ground, but with her bundled state, she barely managed to start the swing going.

"Well," she said with a laugh, "this isn't nearly as much fun as I remembered."

Roth went behind her and took hold of the two ropes that held the swing. "Allow me." He pulled her back with all his strength and let her fly.

She squealed, and he grinned, then pushed against her back as she came closer again, sending her higher still. The dark skirts fluttered under the coat as blue as the sky, until she looked like an eagle soaring through the clouds.

And his heart soared with her.

She was a girl again, before her father had started insisting she behave like him, before her mother had put up her hair and let down her skirts. The worries, the duties, slipped away to be replaced by the simple joy of flying through the air.

And coming back to arms she could trust.

"My turn! My turn!" Audra came running, with Shaw and James not too far behind. Thea put down her feet, felt the ropes catch as Roth must have grabbed them. She slowed, stopped.

Turning, she met his gaze. "Thank you."

He inclined his head. "It was my pleasure."

Hers as well.

She had to force herself to look to her daughter. "You

may each take a turn, if Mr. Roth is willing." She glanced at him again. "But perhaps not quite so high?"

"Mother!" Shaw complained.

"I will be gentle," Roth promised.

And he was. Always. How could someone be so powerful, so masterful, and yet so tender? He let Audra go only as high as Thea was comfortable, pushed James just a little higher than he was comfortable, and let Shaw direct exactly how high he wanted within a safe boundary. She might have to wonder whether Felden would behave as a butler should, if Vernon would bring her a solution rather than a problem, and if Westerbrook would come making demands, but she did not have to worry about Roth.

They returned home in time to clean up and change for dinner, then met in the dining room. The boys were full of questions about the animals, which she did her best to answer. Roth contributed a little as well, though she knew he had not been raised on a farm.

Audra, however, had another object in mind. "Christmas is coming," she said as the footmen served the dessert course of raisins and nuts. "May we have a Yule log, Mother? And decorations? And plum pudding?"

"I suspect plum pudding may have been started, but I will check," Thea said. "Perhaps Nurse Waters will help you make some decorations." She still wasn't sure she was up to the task.

Nurse Waters nodded eagerly. "Mrs. Willoughby will be glad to help as well." Apparently she deemed decorating a more ladylike pursuit than some Audra preferred.

"Do you celebrate Christmas, Mr. Roth?" James asked.

"Even as a boy," Roth told him. "At the silver mines, we would have a Christmas tree for all the workers, and everyone received a treat."

Audra frowned. "What's a Christmas tree?"

"Another way to say Yule Log," Shaw told her condescendingly.

"No," Roth corrected him. "You cut down your Yule log, strip it of its branches, and burn it in the hearth. We cut down a Christmas tree, stand it up in our home, and decorate it with stars and banners."

She'd heard of such a custom. "I believe some of the German states honor this tradition as do some of the House of Hanover."

"Batavaria honors it as well," Roth said. "The woodcutters always vied to bring King Frederick the largest, fullest fir to be given the honor of being erected in the palace. The king continued the tradition when we were in exile. It was a little harder when we were in Italy, but we managed."

"Then we should have one as well," Thea said with a nod.

His smile was her reward.

Thea was well pleased with herself as she finished her correspondence on Monday. Roth's idea of using a flat-bottomed boat to allow workers to open holes in the ice had set the water to flowing down the hillside again, and her tenant had what he needed for his family and animals. Mrs. Willoughby and Nurse Waters had agreed to prepare the house for Christmas. For the first time in a long time, everything felt on course.

"Forgive the interruption, your ladyship," Felden said from the doorway. "But Lord Westerbrook has come. Again."

She felt for her butler. "Put him in the withdrawing room, Felden. I'll join him shortly." She sealed the last of her letters and rose to go see what the fellow wanted this time.

Dressed in a navy coat and fawn-colored trousers, he had been lounging on the sofa closest to the hearth, running his palms along the rose-colored velvet as if relishing it. He popped to his feet as she entered and swept her a bow.

Thea ignored the expansive gesture and went to sit on a chair just out of reach. "Good day, Westerbrook. Here to see the boys?"

"Actually, no," he said. Instead of returning to his seat, he went down on one knee in front of her.

Thea leaned farther back, but he managed to capture one of her hands, pressing it against his wine-colored waistcoat.

"Dear Thea," he said, face turned up entreatingly, "you must know that I have always admired you. But you have been in mourning. It would have been unseemly for me to express my devotion."

Thea tugged out of his grip. "It is unseemly now. My year of mourning doesn't end until January, as you yourself have pointed out."

"Ah, but I could not wait another moment." He gazed at her, brow puckered and eyes turned down, reminding her of a hunting dog her father had once owned. "I am already your sons' guardian. Allow me to be their father. Marry me, Thea."

Only the years of training to be a countess kept her from choking. "You honor me, Westerbrook," she said, pleased by the calm, level tone. "But I must refuse."

"Darling, you need not feel encumbered by the past," he urged her. "Think how happy Thomas would be if he knew I was providing for you."

She had cared for her husband, but she would not marry to please him. "The answer, I fear, is no."

He held up one hand. "Then do not answer me yet." He rose and looked to Felden. Her butler's face was slack, very likely from shock.

"Felden, bring me my wards. I'm sure they have an opinion on the matter."

Thea surged up. "Leave Shaw and James out of this."

He offered her a sad smile. "I fear I cannot. This decision affects their future as well." He looked to the butler again and frowned. "Why are you still here?"

"Milady?" Felden asked, brows up in question.

"Do as he says," she replied, vowing never to agree to anything else.

Felden bowed and left them.

"You needn't behave as if I were your first suitor, you know," Westerbrook said, moving back toward the sofa. "You are a widow. Besides, you understand the need for continuance."

She gritted her teeth behind her smile a moment before sinking back onto the chair. "I have no need for additional continuance, my lord. I have an heir, as does he, in his brother and sister, until he is old enough to wed and sire children of his own. I am sufficient."

"A very happy circumstance, to be sure." He aimed his frown at the door. "Where are they?"

"It is a large castle," Thea reminded him. "It takes a while to move about."

He plopped back down on the sofa with a petulant sigh.

Fortunately for her, he had not renewed his suit before Shaw and James came in. She wasn't sure whether to be relieved or dismayed that Roth accompanied them. He stood beside Felden along the wall, and the two exchanged a look.

"My boys," Westerbrook said, rising to pace before them, "I have become very fond of you. I would like to stand in place of your father, but your mother refuses to marry me."

James blinked. "She can't marry you. She's married to Father."

"She can marry as a widow," Shaw told his brother.

"But I hope she won't." He looked to Thea, who smiled at him.

"Nonsense," Westerbrook said. "Your father would want me to protect you all. I can only do that well if I am married to your mother. I'm sure you'd like a new father, wouldn't you, James?"

"Yes," James admitted, earning him a scowl from Shaw. "But not you."

Westerbrook reddened, then turned to Thea. "I see you have poisoned them against me. I was hoping we could come to an amicable agreement, but it seems you have stolen that chance as well. Duty compels me to protect these boys as Thomas would have wanted. So, you will marry me, or I will send them away for their own good."

"No!" James ran to her arms, and Thea cradled him close.

Shaw stood with head high, meeting the viscount's gaze. "It is beneath you to behave in this manner, my lord."

Westerbrook ignored him. "Well?" he demanded, striding up to Thea. "What is your answer?"

She never had a chance to tell him. He suddenly jerked back from her, like a marionette on strings.

"Time to go, my lord," Roth said, and he twisted the viscount enough that Thea could spot one of Roth's hands on the miscreant's collar and the other on the waist of his trousers, which appeared to be riding unnaturally high.

"Unhand me!" Westerbrook ordered, squirming. "Felden! Remove this man!"

Felden made a face. "Terribly sorry, my lord, but he's an Imperial Guard. I'd never stand a chance."

He actually grinned as Roth hauled the sputtering viscount out.

CHAPTER ELEVEN

JAMES WRAPPED HIS arms about Thea's middle and hugged her tight. Shaw went so far as to come and pat her shoulder.

"Forgive me, my loves," she said, glancing from one to the other. "I simply cannot marry that man."

"We would not want you to, Mother," Shaw told her.

"He's awful," James agreed.

Despite their support, doubts came thundering in, wielding sword and pistol. "But if I don't do as he asks, I very much fear he'll do as he threatened. You must have either a guardian or a father, and, whether I like it or not, Westerbrook is your guardian. Oh, I cannot lose you!"

She gathered Shaw close with her other arm and held them both. They were becoming gentlemen, but for a moment, they were just her little boys, her darlings, their bodies warm against hers. Tears stung her eyes, and she blinked them away.

Please, dear Lord, do not take my sons too!

"Maybe you could marry someone else," James suggested, safe in her arms. "Someone big enough to scare him away."

And, just like that, hope burst free.

Over their heads, she saw Roth returning. He moved calmly to the wall to stand beside Felden, who thumped him on the shoulder before facing front with all the dignity he could pretend.

The will said if she married again, her new husband would become the boys' guardian as well as their father. A husband could help her think through decisions. A husband could protect her sons. A husband could teach them to grow into the gentlemen she knew they could become.

One man was already fulfilling those functions.

Thea released her sons and gave them each an encouraging smile. "I'm sorry Westerbrook's demands troubled you. We will find a way, my loves. Will you go up to the schoolroom? I must speak with Mr. Roth."

James nodded and started for the door. Shaw gave her a puzzled look before following.

"Alone, Felden," she said.

Her butler blinked, then bowed and left them.

Roth eyed her from the other side of the room. "Am I being discharged?"

"No," she said with a laugh that sounded hysterical to her ears. "You might say you're being promoted. Mr. Roth, would you marry me?"

She could not mean that. So many men—any man!—would be a better choice than him.

"Lord Westerbrook's ultimatum upset you," he said. "You will want to think through your options to respond."

"On the contrary," she said, rising. "I have given the matter considerable thought since the day he first threatened me. This is my best option."

He shook his head, but she advanced on him, chin up to meet his gaze. "A husband allows me to remove Lord Westerbrook as guardian for Shaw and James. A husband allows me to remove him from our lives once and for all!" She positively vibrated with the hope of it, and he was reminded of Audra at her most determined.

"Furthermore, having the right husband beside me provides help and advice when I need them. It provides stability for the children and the staff."

"The *right* husband," he agreed. "I am not the right husband."

She stopped in front of him, head cocked. "Why not?" Before he could even answer she was marshalling her arguments, sending them at him like fresh troops into battle.

"Your interactions with the children and me show you to be an honorable man. You have provided me with advice that has proven quite helpful. Your former position guarding the King of Batavaria tells me you are trained to protect. Serving in that position also demonstrates you know how to deal with the aristocracy and royalty."

"But I am not of the aristocracy or royalty," he pointed out. "I am beneath you in all ways."

Her lips thinned. "You are beneath me only in consequence as Society counts such things. And, I can assure you, nearly every man of my acquaintance is in the same position."

Some part of him pushed him to accept. He fought it. "You could marry another earl, a marquess, a duke, or a prince," he suggested instead.

She made a face. "Alas, unmarried men of that standing are few and far between, and even fewer want to marry a widow encumbered with children. Some might even fear me too old to give them an heir."

"Then they are fools," he said.

She pressed a hand to her chest. "And you would have me marry a fool, Mr. Roth?"

"I would have you marry a man who can bring honor to your house."

She pulled back her hand to wave it. "My house has sufficient honor, thank you very much. I would prefer to marry a man I knew I could trust with my children."

She truly was adamant about this. The arguments were logical, well-considered. But she didn't know him.

"What exactly are you proposing, then?" he asked.

"A marriage of convenience," she explained. She spit out the words, as if they had an unpleasant taste. "We will be partners in running my holdings as well as nurturing the children. You will not send them away to school." The flash of her eyes would have had him rethinking that idea, if he had endorsed it in the first place. "The term some use for your position is consort."

He had had worse terms applied to him. "You still give me too much power. Even for a countess in her own right, would not making me your husband give me control of your lands, your income?"

"For anything not entailed, which is a small portion," she admitted. "But I trust you, Mr. Roth."

The honor of it nearly knocked him off his feet, more surely than a pugilist's blow.

"You should not," he said. "Too much is at stake."

She regarded him. "Have you done something dishonorable that would make me rescind my offer?"

He could not say it aloud. He could not give her such a disgust of him. One of the reasons he'd stayed in England was because so few here knew the truth.

"Surely there is someone better suited to the role."

She blew out a breath. "No one. And you heard Westerbrook. Do you think he will wait even a week to make good on his threats? Hilary term of school starts in January. I can assure you he will enroll Shaw and James in it unless I agree to marry him."

The desire to give in mounted with every word. He had been selfish once. He would not fall into that trap again.

"And there is no other way to fight him?" he pressed.

"None. I have considered the matter, at length, from all angles. I had hoped hiring you as tutor would satisfy him." She rubbed a hand up her arm. "Little did I dream he would propose marriage. We have never gotten on particularly well."

"His debts are mounting," he said. "He is desperate."

Her brows rose. "Why, Mr. Roth, how kind of you to praise my character and accomplishments."

"Your beauty, character, and talents need no praise," Roth said. "Which is why I am certain you could do better in a husband than me."

Her sigh was deep and heartfelt. "Have I not been persuasive enough? If you will not consider the good you would be doing the children, consider the gain you might achieve. Besides having access to my income and properties, you would be treated with the respect due the lord of the manor. You need never worry about finding a position, particularly one unworthy of your skills, again. You will have food, shelter, and companionship all the days of your life, with no more effort, nay, likely less effort, than you have now. Surely you see the benefits."

He did. And he knew he did not deserve any of them. But much more of her persuasion, and he would be bowing at her feet. "I will consider the matter," he said.

She smiled, and the entire room sparkled with light. "Thank you, Mr. Roth. I look forward to hearing your decision. Please do not wait too long, however. As I said, Lord Westerbrook will not tarry in enacting his vengeance."

He bowed and left her.

He stalked down the corridor and took the stairs to the top floor two at a time. He wanted to run, to ride, to move.

To escape.

He stopped himself just outside the schoolroom door and took a deep breath. She had honored him beyond all thought, and he had argued beyond endurance. He must give the matter his full attention.

Unfortunately, that proved impossible in his current position, which he seemed to be doing poorly.

"The answer is nine point five," Shaw said after Roth had marked his sums. "James, I have that right, don't I?"

His younger brother eyed the slate, then frowned at Roth. "It seems to be correct. Is there some other theorem, sir?"

Roth shook his head. "No. You are correct. Thank you, Shaw, for noticing."

Shaw also frowned, but nodded.

Roth rose. "Let's collect Lady Audra and see about some boxing lessons. Shaw, you may accompany us this time."

Shaw grinned as he popped up.

But even the physical movement didn't help his concentration. He had just instructed Audra about her jab when she hit him squarely in the stomach. Sucking in a breath, he did his best not to bend.

Her eyes widened. "I thought you would block."

"I *should* have blocked," Roth wheezed out.

"Is something wrong, Mr. Roth?" James asked.

The information should have come from their mother, but he realized he could not answer their mother unless he knew they would be agreeable. He motioned them to the benches along the wall.

"Shaw and James know that Lord Westerbrook threatened to send them away," he started.

Audra smacked her wrapped fists together. "The rat!"

"He thinks it would be best for us," James tried, glancing between his brother and sister.

"What do you think?" Roth asked.

Shaw sighed. "Most young men go to school eventually. I would prefer to stay close to Mother a while longer. She needs us."

James and Audra nodded.

"She thinks she needs a husband as well," Roth said, watching them. "She has asked me to be that husband."

Audra's face brightened. "Oh, good!"

"Excellent choice," James put in.

Shaw said nothing.

"I am inclined to refuse," Roth told them. "I do not wish to take the place of your father."

"Why?" Audra asked.

"Because I am not worthy," Roth told her gently.

"At least you answered that question correctly," Shaw muttered.

"Shaw!" James protested.

"No," Roth said, holding up a hand, "he's right. I am not the kind of gentleman your mother deserves."

"I like you," Audra said. Her hopeful gaze kindled something inside him, a candle flickering in the dark.

"I like you too," James said, head up a bit defiantly, and the candle brightened. James looked to Shaw.

"I think Mother knows what she's doing," the oldest boy said. "You should marry her."

Roth stared at him, then glanced at the others. "You are in agreement?"

They all nodded.

The candle roared into a fire, burning through the last of his objections. He rose on shaky legs. "Then I suppose I should go tell your mother the good news."

She had asked her sons' tutor to marry her.

Seated at her desk in the library, Thea set down the quill after dripping ink on the paper for the third time. It didn't matter what correspondence she needed to attend to or what she must review from Mr. Vernon or Mrs. Willoughby. Her mind could only grasp one thing.

Roth was upstairs now, deciding whether to link his life to hers.

Forever.

She pushed back from the desk. What had she been thinking? He was right. It was impossible. The children would never accept him as a father. The staff would find the entire idea preposterous. Her neighbors would be shocked, her friends scandalized. She wasn't even out of mourning yet!

Someone rapped on the door.

"Come in, Felden," she said before remembering that her butler sometimes forgot such niceties.

Roth stepped into the room. His face was tighter than his broad shoulders, his lips a sharp slash across his face.

"Forgive me," she said, rising. "I should never have…"

"I agree," he said.

Thea plopped down on the chair so hard she nearly winced. "Oh, well, then."

He moved closer, strength and purpose advancing on her. "Forgive the presumption, but I spoke with Shaw, James, and Audra. They agree with your plan. With their blessing and for their sakes, I will marry you."

She should be incensed he'd speak to the children ahead of her, but he seemed to understand them better than she did lately. And it seemed they trusted him too. She managed a deep breath. "That's settled, then. All that remains are the appropriate arrangements."

"Have Nurse Waters watch the children the rest of the day and tomorrow morning," he said. "I will ride to London for a special license. I will likely need to spend the night there. We can be married tomorrow afternoon."

So soon? Well, yes, of course so soon. She'd told him they needed to make all haste. Lord Westerbrook was breathing out his dire threats.

"Very wise," she said.

He nodded to the desk. "Write down your full name, date of birth, and parish of record. That is what Count Montalban needed to secure a special license to marry Lady Calantha."

The fresh piece of parchment rattled as she set it in place. She could only hope he wouldn't notice. It took all her concentration to write the particulars in a hand the Archbishop's staff would actually be able to read.

"I believe there is a fee," she said, head down over her work. "I'll have Mrs. Willoughby pull it from the household account."

"No need." His tone was as terse as the two words. "I can pay."

She had insulted him. She managed to finish the last of the information, sanded the paper, then handed it to him. Their gazes brushed.

"Thank you," she said.

His face finally softened. "I should be the one to thank you." He folded the paper into his jacket, then met her gaze again. "You will make the arrangements with the minister?"

Mr. Bloomsberg would be stunned, but she had the power over his living, so he would likely agree. "Yes, of course."

He inclined his head and turned for the door, then looked back. "If possible, I would like Lady Belfort and Mr. Keller to attend. Mr. Tanner is on his honeymoon, and Mr. Huber, the other guard in our group, would not be able to reach us in time."

"I will write to them this moment," she promised.

He nodded and left her.

And just like that, she was engaged. Again.

She shook her head. Last time it had taken months to plan her wedding. Her friends and acquaintances had called to congratulate her. Her mother had made appointments with the finest modiste in London to craft the wedding clothes. Thomas's mother had insisted on feting her at teas and a ball. None of that would be possible this time.

As it was, she barely had time to choose a gown!

She spent the next little while penning missives to have a footman deliver. She took some pleasure in informing Westerbrook that he no longer needed to concern himself with being guardian of her sons, picturing his face when he learned of her marriage too late to stop it. But she did not like thinking how Meredith would react on hearing that Thea had promptly married the man sent to tutor her sons. She wasn't even ready to explain everything to the staff, yet Felden at the very least must know the truth of it.

"You were witness to Lord Westerbrook's tirade earlier," she told him when he attended her in the library.

Her butler nodded. "A shameful display, if I may say so, your ladyship."

"Indeed, and a rather frightening one, given the power his guardianship has over me. So, I have decided to negate that power. I will be marrying again."

Felden started, then grinned at her. "And who is the lucky fellow, milady?"

"Mr. Roth."

He tapped one ear. "Forgive me, Lady Alldene, but I could have sworn you said Mr. Roth."

"I did say Mr. Roth. He is trained to protect, used to dealing with the aristocracy, and good with the children."

He scratched his ear as if he still wasn't sure he was hearing correctly. "So, why did he ride out just now as if a flea had bit him?"

That must look suspicious indeed. "He is going for a special license. We will be married tomorrow afternoon, if Mr. Bloomsberg agrees."

"Well, then," he said, "I guess all I can say is congratulations, your ladyship."

She had a feeling others would have a great many more things to say about the matter.

CHAPTER TWELVE

SOMEONE HAD FOLLOWED him from the castle. Roth hadn't been sure until he had passed Weybridge. Most would have turned off there. This fellow kept coming, but far enough back that it was clear he didn't intend to catch up, as he would if Thea had sent him with a message for Roth. Roth nearly stopped to demand an explanation, but his mission was too important. He urged Thea's horse into a canter.

He reached London late that afternoon and was just in time to speak to the clerks at Doctors' Commons, the location where the Archbishop of Canterbury had decreed to secure special licenses. The request was rare enough that he was sent to a private office to one side, where the head clerk came with paper, ink, and quill.

"I trust you have already spoken with His Grace?" he asked in a high-pitched voice, dipping the quill in the ink.

"Is that necessary?" Roth returned from the other side of the polished wood table.

The fellow glanced up. He was small and slender, like an elf clutching his writings close. "Not entirely. So long as His Grace would recognize your family name."

The Archbishop of Canterbury would have to travel widely indeed to know of the Roth family of Batavaria. He raised his chin. "He will not recognize my family name, but he will recognize the names of my previous employer and my patroness."

The fellow waited expectantly.

"I previously served Prince Otto Leopold of the Principality of Batavaria and soon the Ambassador to the Court of St. James from Württemberg. My patroness in England is Lady Belfort."

He blinked, and Roth could not tell if it was from surprise or awe. "And they will vouch for you?" Now he sounded suspicious.

"The prince is currently in Württemberg ratifying the agreement between your great kingdom and his. Lady Belfort resides in Surrey."

The clerk clucked his tongue. "Good sir, I must be able to attest to His Grace that you are a man who will honor his word. Will no one in London witness your bond?"

Roth rose, standing tall as he'd been taught, shoulders back, head high, feet braced. "I, Stephen Roth, captain in the Batavaria Imperial Guard, hand chosen to serve King Frederick these last ten years, do hereby give you my bond that everything I say is right and true."

The clerk stared up at him a moment, then bent over the paper again. "I will need the name, age, occupation, and marital status of each of the parties."

Roth nearly sagged with relief, but he did not let the fellow see it. Instead, he deigned to sit and pulled out the paper with Thea's particulars. At least he had the money to pay the cost and Stamp Duty when the fellow finished inscribing the long piece of paper. He smiled remembering her offer to pay.

Then his smile faded as he recalled his situation. Soon, he would earn no money of his own. He would only have hers. And he vowed to be a good steward of her trust.

The sun was setting as he came out of Doctors' Commons. Though it had taken him only two hours to reach the place, he didn't dare ride back to the castle in the dark. He and the other Imperial Guards had stayed at a hotel along the Strand when they'd first come to London with the king. He appealed to the proprietors, who gladly gave him a room for the night. But he hadn't even started up the stairs to his room before he was hailed across the spacious lobby.

"Mr. Roth."

The friendly tone didn't sway him, not when he'd most recently heard that voice raised in demand.

"My lord," he said, inclining his head to Lord Westerbrook, who strolled closer, looking ready for the evening in his black velvet cloak and black trousers. Roth should probably have bowed, but the man certainly didn't warrant it, no matter his position.

"What a happy circumstance to find you here," Westerbrook said. "Come. Let me treat you to a drink."

Roth didn't move. "I am not thirsty. Thank you."

"Dinner, then," Westerbrook tried. "I have a proposition for you."

"I am not interested." He turned for the stairs.

"Come now," Westerbrook said, pacing him though it clearly took a little effort. "Just a word then. Man to man."

"We are one man short," Roth replied.

Westerbrook chuckled, completely missing the point. "You always were the humble one. I'd like to hire you as a bodyguard. One hundred pounds a month."

It was an exorbitant fee. Imperial Guards didn't make half as much. Whole families lived well on one hundred pounds a year.

"Not interested," Roth repeated. "Rumor has it you cannot afford the price, and I have a better position."

His friendly façade cracked at last. "What?" he sneered. "Will you go back to guarding your little steam works when I send the boys for a proper education? Or perhaps Lady Alldene requires someone to shovel out her stables."

"Lady Alldene requires a husband," he said. "We marry tomorrow."

Lord Westerbrook gaped. Roth left him that way.

He rarely traveled without his pistol and knives. He kept both at the ready that evening. Westerbrook wouldn't have the courage to face him directly, but he could hire a lot of evil with a hundred pounds. Still, no one troubled him, and he left the hotel early the next morning for Alldene Castle.

Only to find someone behind him again.

He was likely the same fellow who had followed Roth to London and just as likely to be in Westerbrook's employ. It was the best explanation for why the viscount had appeared at the hotel. The fellow had followed Roth to the hotel and run to his master, and Westerbrook had arrived in time to attempt to hire Roth. Was this fellow now intending to spy on Thea? Or worse?

The best road from London to Alldene ran through Walton-on-Thames down toward Weybridge, but he knew the River Road that passed Rose Hill, Lady Belfort's estate, would eventually intersect with the Weybridge Road again after crossing the River Wey. Accordingly, he guided the horse onto the River Road and spurred him into a gallop. They thundered past the estate and down to where the road turned away from the Thames. Roth slowed the horse to a trot, then stopped under the shadows of a hedgerow. He counted to fifteen before his follower came along the road.

Roth guided the horse into the light. "Looking for me?"

The fellow reined in. He was tall and lanky, with a sharp nose and narrow eyes. "I'm not looking for trouble, that's for certain," he declared in a gravelly voice.

"You've found it nonetheless." Roth drew his pistol and aimed it at the man's breast. "State your purpose, or turn around and keep out of my sight."

The fellow jerked on the reins, turned the horse, and disappeared back down the River Road toward Weyton.

Roth continued on to the castle. He kept glancing behind but caught no sign of his follower.

That didn't mean the fellow was gone. He may have found a less obvious way to watch Roth and Thea. Best to show his lordship that his time of terror was over.

"Perhaps some pearls in your hair, milady?" Martin suggested.

Thea gazed at herself in the mirror. She'd chosen a dinner dress of a powdered blue nearly the color of her eyes, with a darker blue ribbon crossing her chest and adorning the hem in graceful swags. Her maid had piled her hair in a complicated set of braids and curls, with little tendrils brushing Thea's cheeks, which had entirely too little color.

"This should suffice," she replied. "It isn't as if he's going to run back to Batavaria at the sight of me."

Martin tsked. "Certainly not. He's a most fortunate fellow."

She could only hope he had come to see it that way.

And she could only hope he would come back!

She'd given Felden strict instructions to send word the moment Roth returned to the castle. Meredith had written to say that she, Fortune, and Mr. Keller would be here by half-past two. The elegant hand and kind tone betrayed no shock in the sudden announcement. If only Mr. Bloomsberg had reacted as well.

"A wedding at the castle, Lady Alldene?" her minister had queried when she'd met with him at the vicarage yesterday afternoon. She'd thought coming in person rather than sending a note might make him more amenable to agreeing. "Who is marrying?"

"I am," she said.

His snowy brows rose. "Indeed. Has the time of mourning passed so quickly, then?"

"We have three more weeks," she replied, "but I believe Thomas would be glad to see me settled."

"Assuredly," he agreed. "And who is the gentleman?"

"Mr. Stephen Roth."

He blinked. "Mr. Roth? The tutor?"

"Mr. Roth, the former Batavarian Imperial Guardsman, praised throughout the Continent for his courage and fortitude," she countered. "Highly decorated for his efforts to safeguard his kingdom from Napoleon's predations. A leader of men."

"I…see." He adjusted his spectacles. "This is highly unusual. I will draw up the banns."

"No need," she said. "Mr. Roth has ridden to London for a special license. We would like to be married at three of the hour tomorrow."

He choked. "Tomorrow!"

"Tomorrow, in the castle chapel. I will expect to see you there."

She'd swept out before he could question her further.

The rumors were no doubt already swirling. Why would the countess marry before her time of mourning was over? Had she thought so little of her first husband? And why the rush to wed? Had she done something that warranted a hurried betrothal?

And to marry her sons' tutor!

The scandal would follow her for years. She drew in a fortifying breath. It would be worth the scandal if it kept her sons safe from Westerbrook's influence.

There was a rap at the door now. Thea tensed, and Martin went to answer it.

"Lady Belfort and Mr. Keller have arrived with her ladyship's cat," Felden said from the corridor. "I took the liberty of escorting them to the chapel. Nurse Waters will bring down the children shortly."

"And Mr. Roth?" Thea pressed, swiveling to face him fully.

"Will be here any moment, I'm sure, your ladyship," Felden promised her.

She nodded, and he left.

Had Roth taken the opportunity to escape her mad request and hide away at Rose Hill? No, surely Meredith would not have come had he reappeared at her door seeking another position.

She rose. Martin came back to her side and offered her a smile. "You look lovely, milady."

"Good enough to wed," she joked.

"Good enough to ascend the throne," Martin argued.

The second knock had them both turning. Felden came in unbidden.

"He's back," he said, smile broad. "I will help him prepare. I suggest you go to the chapel to await him."

Thea nodded, though she knew it was shaky.

"My very best wishes, your ladyship," Martin warbled as Thea headed for the door. "May your new marriage be even more blessed than the first."

Oh, how she wanted to hope!

The chapel had seen hundreds of marriages, baptisms, and funerals over the centuries the castle had stood. Somehow, she didn't think it had witnessed a wedding quite like this. Dark wood paneling carved with roses covered every wall, with barely enough room left for a stained glass window depicting the Christ child. Normally, the simple wood benches were only sufficient to accommodate her and her immediate family, but Felden had crammed in a few more. James and Audra were sitting with Nurse Waters on the front bench, with Meredith and Mr. Keller just behind. Two grey ears poking up over the shoulder of her friend's lavender gown told Thea that Fortune was also in residence. But where was Shaw?

Her oldest son stepped out of the shadows near the back of the room. He was dressed in the black suit he had worn to his father's funeral, though he had adapted a white shirt and cravat. Her little man!

"Shaw?" she asked.

"I am told it is customary for the gentleman head of the family to give the bride in marriage," he said solemnly. He offered her his arm. "May I, Mother?"

He would make her cry. She could only nod and set her hand on his.

Shaw walked with her with measured tread up to the minister, who nodded his thanks. As her son went to sit with his siblings, Mr. Bloomsberg peered at her through his spectacles. "And the groom?"

"Apologizes for being late."

She turned. Roth stood in the doorway in a black jacket with gold braid spanning his chest. It must be his dress uniform from his time as an Imperial Guard. Oh, but he must have intimidated them all with one look. Head high, he marched down the aisle to join her. Thea smiled.

He did not.

She looked back at the minister to find him gazing at her groom in obvious awe.

"Mr. Bloomsberg?" she asked.

He shook himself and hurriedly opened his Book of Common Prayer.

"Dearly beloved, we are gathered together here in the sight of God," he began.

He continued reading the words she had heard at the marriage of family and friends, most recently Julia Hewett's. What struck Thea was how different this felt from her first marriage. Her father had given her away. Now, when the minister asked, "Who giveth this woman to be married to this man?" Shaw stood up, chin up, and said, "I do."

Roth nodded his thanks.

Thomas had rattled off the expected responses as if hoping to speed the ceremony. Roth responded to the questions deliberately in his firm, strong voice. Such confidence. Such command. She would never have to fear again.

There was great comfort in that.

Thomas had smiled and winked at her when she'd forgotten part of the long recitation of duties and obligations. No one had to remind her to say her vows this time. She matched Roth's confidence, if not his presence. And when Mr. Bloomsberg finished his admonitions, she turned to look at her family and friends with every hope for a happy future.

They looked back.

Waiting.

She glanced at Roth. He returned their looks with no emotion whatsoever. She glanced at Mr. Bloomsberg, who was also waiting.

The minister cleared his throat. "I believe, in some circles, it is customary…that is some husbands find it prudent to…ah…kiss the bride."

"No," Roth said, and he took her hand, tucked it in his arm, and led her out of the chapel.

Nurse Waters took Shaw, James, and Audra to the dining room, where an early dinner would be served. It had seemed the least she could do for those who had come on such short notice. The rest of them adjourned for a moment to the library. Mr. Bloomsberg had Mr. Keller and Meredith serve as witnesses, signing their names to the parish marriage register, which he had brought with him, after Thea and Roth had signed. As she waited, she felt her skirts move. Fortune wound around her as if offering a blessing.

"She is well pleased with herself," Meredith said, coming to retrieve her pet. "I think she hoped from the first that you and Roth would make a match of it."

Thea stared at her. "You knew?"

"Fortune knew." She rubbed her cheek against her pet's fur. "She's had a hand in any number of matches over the years."

Her mind boggled.

Still, it was a surprisingly merry dinner. As if to celebrate with them, her cook had gone out of her way to offer some of Thea's favorites, including pheasant in a spicy sauce made with apricots from their hot houses and a mincemeat tart.

Mr. Bloomsberg left first after offering his congratulations in such a wondering tone that she thought he was still questioning her decision. Meredith and Mr. Keller left next, after a reminder of the upcoming Christmas Eve party, so as to be back to her estate before dark. Nurse Waters hustled the children up to the schoolroom without once looking at Roth.

Thea and her new husband sat on opposite sides of the withdrawing room. In the silence, she could hear a coal settling in the hearth.

"Shall I call you Stephen?" she asked.

"I have always been addressed by my last name," he replied. "Would it please you to have me call you Lady Alldene or Thea?"

Truly, could they be any more awkward? It was as if they had just started courting instead of having pledged their lives to each other. "Thea, please."

He nodded, leaning back in the chair. "You should be aware that Westerbrook knows we have wed."

Thea frowned. "How? I wrote him, but he likely won't receive the note until tomorrow."

"He has someone watching the castle. The man

followed me to London and back, and Westerbrook showed up at my hotel."

Her body tightened with each word. "Did he accost you?"

He snorted as if the idea was laughable, and she supposed it was. Roth might not be able to strike back as a commoner, but he would know how to defend himself.

"He attempted to hire me," he explained. "I told him I had a far better position, at your side. Perhaps that will be enough to send him into a retreat."

She wasn't sure if it was hope or dread that pushed her to her feet, but she went to the hearth and picked up the poker. The metal felt cool and solid in her grasp. If only the world felt so solid.

Roth joined her silently. Gently taking the poker from her hand, he stirred the coals to life.

"Will you always do that?" she murmured. "Step in to help even when I'm not yet sure I need it?"

"It would be my great honor," he replied. "Do you need anything else this evening, Thea?"

She met his gaze. Those dark eyes watched, waiting. Hoping?

She licked her lips. "No, I suppose not."

"Then I bid you good night."

He bowed and left her.

She wasn't sure how long she stood before the fire, but, at length, she also retired. Martin helped her change for bed, but her maid's fingers seemed to be shaking.

"Is anything wrong, Martin?" she asked.

Martin lowered her voice. "I'm just mindful of your new husband, milady. I don't want to disrupt his plans for the night."

Her stomach flipped. "Very thoughtful of you."

Her maid finished and hurried out.

Of course her efficient servants would have moved him from the tutor's room to the master's suite, which adjoined her own. He was on the other side of that wall, the other side of that door. She had only to call to fetch him to her side.

Thea lay on her bed, sleepless, for a long time, but she did not call.

CHAPTER THIRTEEN

HE WAS MARRIED. The idea refused to sink in. It floated like a leaf on a pond, foreign, disconnected. He was married.

To a countess.

"We will need to hire you a valet, sir," Felden said as he helped Roth off with his shoes that evening. The butler had transferred all of Roth's things from the little room at the top of the stairs near the schoolroom to the master's suite on the chamber story.

"I have never required help before," Roth told him, flexing his newly freed toes against the gold medallions woven into the thick blue carpet.

"You were never lord of the manor," Felden pointed out as he took the shoes to the door, likely for cleaning and polishing before morning. "There will be expectations."

He didn't know which sounded worse: being considered the lord of the manor or the expectations that went with it.

Felden came back to eye him. "Perhaps a shave?"

Roth rubbed his jaw. "It can wait until morning."

"Can it?" The butler tipped his head toward a door in the far paneled wall.

A door that likely led to Thea's bedchamber.

"That will be all, Felden," Roth said.

Felden nodded. "Very good, sir. Just know that I have

spoken to the staff. I expect no difficulties from your elevation, but if you encounter any, you have only to let me know, and I will see the matter settled." He bowed and left.

Alone in the silence, Roth removed his dress uniform and shirt, then pulled on the nightshirt that lay waiting on the brocaded bedcover. He put his clothes away in the wardrobe. It was a massive walnut affair, carved with flowers like almost every other piece of wood furniture and paneling in the castle. It looked nearly empty with his few things inside.

The entire room looked a bit empty as he padded back toward the bed. The bedstead was also carved, though it had no canopy or hangings. The grey stone hearth even had sculpted pillars that resembled Grecian vases containing roses. But once again, despite all the flowers, the hearth was surmounted by a tapestry showing knights marching off to battle. Had the previous lord of the manor appreciated such things, or had someone brought in the piece thinking it would appeal to him?

It did appeal. He could almost picture himself young again, eager to prove himself in the coming fight against France, hoping to regain his honor, his pride.

Never had he dreamed he'd marry so far above his station.

The door in the far wall whispered to him that his wife lay waiting. His charming, cultured, clever, kind wife.

He would not heed the call.

He marched himself to the great bed, jerked back the covers, and settled himself to sleep between the fine sheets.

But it was a long time before he slept. In fact, he thought he'd only been asleep for an hour or so when he caught the sound of someone else in the room. Halting footsteps crossed the floor. James's ghost? Roth kept his breathing steady as the furtive noises moved closer. Then he threw back the covers and leapt from the bed, crouched and fists ready.

Hartshorn, one of the under footmen, stared at him, coal scuttle in one gloved hand. A scuttle that had started to shake.

"Sorry, sir," he stammered. "I was just making up the fire. Do you need help dressing?"

Roth rose to his full height. "No. Thank you. It is morning, then?"

The fellow's nod was equally shaky, and he finished his work so quickly Roth felt the breeze of his passing as the door shut behind him.

The high and mighty lord of the manor, disconcerted by his own servant. He snorted.

When he had been only the boys' tutor, he had either eaten his breakfast with the staff or taken a tray in his room. Now he would likely be expected to eat at the table with his wife. Hartshorn must have reported that he needed no help, for Felden didn't come to assist him in dressing. Wearing his navy coat and chamois trousers, he descended the stairs to the dining room, only to find it empty. Returning to the entry hall, he eyed the blond-haired footman, Griggs, who stood taller.

"Have I missed breakfast?" Roth asked.

Griggs tugged down on his black tailcoat. "No, my lord, that is, sir. It is served in the breakfast room."

"Which is where?" Roth asked.

"Allow me to escort you, sir."

It was on the first story, tucked away near his new bedchamber. He didn't think he or the children had searched it yet. He would have to put it on the list, even though the cozy room with its dark paneling, carved sideboard, round table, and yellow-upholstered high-back chairs had few hiding places. The portraits of various noble personages beamed down benevolently.

Gowned in a frilly white affair he would not have

thought for her, Thea was seated at one side of the round table, sipping from a cup patterned with delicate yellow flowers, which she lowered as he came closer. "Good morning, Mr., er Roth."

"Thea." Had that name come out in a purr? He cleared his throat before going to help himself to the food on the sideboard. It seemed they fed the countess less than the children, for the sideboard held only a partially full rack of toast, pots of jams, and a decanter that contained a thick, sweet-smelling treacle that was likely melted chocolate. He loaded a plate with what he could and went to sit directly opposite her.

She regarded her food.

He ate his.

"You could sit beside me," she ventured. "It's difficult to converse so far apart."

He picked up his plate and carried it to a spot on her left. "As you wish."

Yet she did not converse; she merely watched him over her cup. Carter, the head footman, came in with more toast, and Roth beckoned him closer. "Coffee? And at least three eggs, hard-boiled or scrambled."

"Right away, sir!" He strode out.

"I should have thought to ask," she murmured. "Of course you would want more than what I generally eat for breakfast."

He shrugged, slathering his toast with raspberry preserves. "Easily rectified."

She swirled her cup and said nothing.

He set aside his knife. "Is something wrong?"

"No, nothing," she assured him, setting down her cup again. "Forgive me. I haven't had company at table since..."

"Since your husband died," he surmised.

"My husband," she said, meeting his gaze at last, "is very much alive."

He couldn't help smiling at that. And when she smiled back, every mouthful of the dry toast was ambrosia.

"What do you need of me today?" he asked, as Carter returned with a platter of eggs and a plate of ham that had likely been intended for the staff. Knowing the cook could quickly make more, Roth nodded his thanks and dug in.

"Mr. Vernon and I will be discussing our current tenants and whether one in particular will need to be evicted." Her sigh said how little she was looking forward to the discussion. "You could sit in and provide advice."

He inclined his head. "I would be honored."

She picked up her toast, though it had to have gone cold by now. "And I suppose we will need to find another tutor for the boys."

"No," Roth said, forking up another mouthful. "I can still fulfill that duty."

She cocked her head. "You want to teach my sons?"

He swallowed. "I suppose they are now our sons. As their legal father, I would want to be certain they have all the knowledge and skills to make their way in the world. I may not completely understand the role Shaw must one day take, but I know you will school him there."

Her lashes fluttered. "You astound me."

Was that a tear in her eye? Roth shifted, the chair suddenly hard. "It is only what I would want from my own father, had he lived."

"Of course."

"There will come a time, however," he forced himself to say, "when they will need more tutelage than I can provide."

"We will discuss the matter when that time comes," she replied. "Until then, know that you have my gratitude for your care of them. Perhaps, after breakfast, we could speak to them about it."

Roth nodded.

Audra and the boys were all in the schoolroom when they went up a short while later. Nurse Waters was attempting to get the boys to clean up their latest lead soldier campaign, which stretched across a good portion of the room. Her face pinched when she met Roth's gaze, but she kept her lips closed. What could she say? He was now her employer.

Thea sat at the worktable, and the children gathered around her on the benches. Roth stood behind her. Nurse Waters attempted to fade into the paneling.

"We wanted to speak with you," Thea told the children. "We took a big step yesterday, and some changes will be needed."

Shaw stiffened. "Are you sending us away to school?"

Thea started. "What? No! We married to prevent that from happening."

The boy relaxed a little.

James's hands were worrying in front of his jacket. "Are we getting another tutor?"

"No," Roth answered for her. "It is my honor to teach you. That has not changed."

James dropped his hands and took a deep breath.

"Can I be taught?" Audra asked, glancing between her mother and him. "I'm part of the family too."

"Oh, sweetheart." Thea gathered her closer. "We've talked about this. You're still so young."

"Not so young that I cannot adapt the lessons to include her," Roth offered.

Nurse Waters' head came up, lips pressed tight and eyes flashing.

Thea must have noticed as well, for she smiled at the nurse. "Perhaps we can work out an arrangement. Nurse Waters can continue to care for you and ensure you know everything you need to know as a young lady."

The nurse snapped a nod.

"And Roth can teach you things young ladies

don't always learn—mathematics, history, and natural philosophy."

"And boxing," Audra said, eyes shining.

"Yes, and boxing," Thea agreed with a laugh.

"What are we to call you, then?" Shaw put in. Once again, his voice rang with challenge.

Thea turned her head to glance back at Roth.

"Roth will do," he said. "Perhaps one day I will earn the title of father."

Shaw nodded, but the look in his eyes said he doubted that very much, and Roth could not tell him he felt the same way.

Thea had thought explaining her new circumstances to the children might be the most difficult part of her arrangement with Roth. She had also felt it incumbent upon her to speak to the staff, but Felden had forestalled her.

"No need, milady," her butler had assured her. "Everyone wishes you and Mr. Roth the very best."

Her steward was less enthusiastic. As they gathered to discuss the tenant issue, Vernon kept glancing between them as if he could not fathom why Roth had been invited.

"Mr. Vernon," Thea said. "I do not believe you have met Mr. Roth."

He tipped his chin at Roth. "The children's tutor, I was told."

"Mr. Roth was a distinguished member of the Batavarian Imperial Guard," she said. "He and I married yesterday."

In the act of removing some papers from his satchel, Vernon froze. "Beg pardon?"

"Mr. Roth and I are married," she repeated, wishing

her face didn't feel so hot. "He will be joining us for our discussions from now onward."

Vernon's jaw was as hard as iron. "As you wish, milady." He laid the papers out on her desk in precise order, never once looking at Roth.

"As you can see, all our tenant farms have produced a harvest that might be expected, given weather conditions, for the last three years," Vernon explained. "All that is, except for the lands Mr. Harvey has." He stabbed at a column on his sheet with his finger.

Thea bent closer and felt Roth doing the same. "And he has equal access to water, seed, fertilizer?" Thea asked.

"Identical, milady. In fact, we have made improvements at his farm so he can access water more easily."

Thea frowned. "Has he no explanation?"

Vernon retrieved his finger. "He claims he has been short-handed, yet he makes no effort to resolve the situation."

"Then assign him workers," Roth said, straightening. "Many men would be glad for a position where they are fed and housed. If he cannot train them or they complain of his treatment, you will know he is the problem. If together they cannot manage the farm, you may have to look deeper into the land."

Thea smiled at him. "An excellent suggestion, Roth. Thank you."

"Your father would not have given Harvey such leeway," Vernon complained, gathering up his papers. "He knew when to turn a tenant out."

"It is winter, Mr. Vernon," Thea said, guilt tugging. "We cannot consider ourselves to have done our Christian duty if we turn a man and his family out into the cold."

"That may be what he's banking on," Vernon pointed out.

"In my experience," Roth said quietly, "a man will do much to prevent his family from freezing and starving."

He looked to Thea. "Would you like me to have a word with this farmer?"

Vernon crammed his papers into his satchel. "No need. That's my role. If you're settled on a path of charity then, I will say nothing further about the matter." His jaw was once more so tight she wondered he could get a word out. "With Christmas in a few days, shall we plan to meet after the new year?"

Thea readily agreed, glad to see the last of him. As soon as he was out the door, she turned to Roth. "I have never heard Vernon so disrespectful. I'm sorry you were subjected to that, Roth."

"He will become accustomed to me," Roth replied.

"He had better," Thea said. "Or we may need to find another steward."

But Vernon wasn't the only one shocked by her sudden marriage. That very afternoon, Felden came to find her. She'd gone up to the schoolroom with Roth and was listening to Shaw and James practice French with Audra. Her butler smiled apologetically at the interruption.

"Three of the local ladies have come calling, your ladyship. I wasn't sure if you were receiving."

In other circumstances, she would be on her honeymoon, when it was customary to leave the happy couple alone for a time. Between her odd marriage and the upcoming holidays, her neighbors might justifiably think she'd be willing to visit so soon. Or perhaps they didn't know she had married.

"I will see them, Felden," she said, rising from the worktable. "Audra, come with me. You can see how young ladies entertain themselves."

Her daughter slipped her hand in Thea's, and they ventured down to the withdrawing room.

Few members of the aristocracy lived near Alldene Castle, but her father had always made a point of welcoming the local gentry, and she had done the same.

Mrs. Winfield was the wife of a local squire, who were both well-fed, well-read individuals. The widowed Mrs. Latterly and her recently out daughter, Frances, lived in a small manor just north of the village. With their soft brown hair and wide blue eyes, they looked like a pair of porcelain-headed dolls. The three ladies smiled as Thea had Audra make her curtseys.

"And is everyone ready for Christmas?" Thea asked politely as Felden sent a footman for tea.

Mrs. Winfield rested her hands on the shimmering blue lustring fabric that strained against her stomach. "Plum pudding being stirred and goose being plucked this very afternoon."

"We had thought to have venison," Mrs. Latterly said. "But it is so difficult to find these days. Didn't I say as much, Francis?"

"You did, Mama," her daughter said dutifully, and Thea found she preferred Audra's enthusiasm.

Mrs. Latterly turned her gaze on Thea. "And what will your new husband expect, Lady Alldene? I heard he is German."

"Pork sausages and pickled cabbage, no doubt," Mrs. Winfield said with a nod.

"Mr. Roth is Batavarian, not German," Thea explained. "And he has already been telling us about his family traditions."

"I've been making red, green, and white paper stars for the Christmas tree," Audra supplied with a proud smile.

"Never heard of such things," Mrs. Winfield declared. "But then again, you have to learn a great deal when you marry so quickly."

"Marry at haste," Mrs. Latterly said, though she was wise enough not to finish the old saying in Thea's presence.

"Will we have a chance to meet this Mr. Roth?" Mrs. Winfield asked, glancing at the door as if hoping he'd pop into view any moment.

"You will have seen him at services," Thea replied. "He has attended the last three weeks."

Mrs. Latterly frowned. "I do not recall anyone else in your pew."

"Mr. Roth sits in the gallery," Thea replied. She would not mention that he sat with the footmen.

Now Mrs. Winfield frowned too. "The impossibly imposing dark-haired fellow? I thought he was your sons' tutor."

"He's a very good tutor," Audra piped up. "He's teaching me to box."

"Ah, there's the tea," Thea said as Felden and the footman brought in the tray. "Let me pour for you, ladies, and you can tell me all about your plans for the new year."

Somehow, she managed to make it through the visit, and Felden saw the ladies out.

Audra swung her hand as they climbed the stairs. "That was nice, Mother. But I like boxing better. Will you watch me?"

"Perhaps we could work on those decorations first," Thea said with a smile.

Audra gave a little skip as they came out onto the landing. "Would you make one of the pretty balls you made last year, with the winter roses and ribbons? We could hang it in the entry hall."

Thea nearly missed a step. "A kissing bough? Who would use it?"

"I could kiss you on the cheek," Audra offered. She cast her a glance. "And you could kiss our new father."

Kiss Roth? Would she ever dare?

CHAPTER FOURTEEN

ROTH WATCHED AS Thea sat at the worktable in the schoolroom, graceful hands knitting together pieces of ribbon and evergreen. The scent of the boughs drifted through the room, a touch of Christmas come early. She had changed from the frilly white morning dress to a rose-colored gown with a white ruff that framed her face.

He tried to keep his gaze there, but it was impossible not to notice the rows of gathered flounces. They edged the wide collar two deep and ran along the overskirt in rows of three. Worse was the single row that outlined her bosom. A man could go mad following those curves.

Better to focus on her presence. The whole room felt brighter, lighter. The children bloomed, voices happy, bodies relaxed. It wasn't the upcoming celebration. She was good for them.

She was good for him too.

He would not dwell on that. He had been given the greatest of gifts, totally undeserved. Right now, he just wanted to enjoy it.

Shaw shifted closer to him on the bench with a glance down the table to where Nurse Waters was helping Audra. "We still have to search the library," he murmured.

"And the breakfast room," Roth murmured back.

Shaw nodded. "We won't be able to break away

before dinner with Mother here. Can you come with us tonight?"

"I will join you after dinner," Roth promised.

He seemed to accept that.

Audra set down the paper she had been cutting. "When may we box?"

Nurse Waters' face settled into forbidding lines. Roth ignored her.

"When you are finished with your decorations," he said. Thea glanced up, and belatedly he realized he should have let her take the lead. "That is, if your mother approves."

"I approve," she said with a smile.

Nurse Waters sighed.

And so, a short time later, they all adjourned to the practice room. Roth helped Audra wrap her hands while James helped Shaw. Roth was assisting James with his when Audra stalked into the middle of the room and raised her fists. "I'm ready, Shaw."

Roth stiffened. So did Thea.

"I thought Audra was only to practice with James," she said with a look to Roth.

"That was my instruction," Roth replied.

Shaw strutted out to his sister. "I don't mind teaching her a lesson."

Roth took a step forward, but before he could separate the two, Audra thrust out her arm. She connected with her brother's chin, and he collapsed to the floor.

Thea rushed forward. "Shaw!"

Roth caught Audra in his arms and drew her back. She looked not the least contrite about the blow. Her dark eyes were narrowed on her brother, and her little frame vibrated, as if she couldn't wait to strike him again.

Shaw put out a hand to hold Thea off. "I'm fine, Mother." He climbed slowly to his feet, and Roth waited for the explosion. By the tension in Thea's shoulders, she was doing the same.

"That wasn't fair, Audra," Shaw said, rubbing his chin with one wrapped hand. "I wasn't ready."

"Then I'll beat you again," Audra replied, wiggling in Roth's hold.

"No, you will not," Thea said. "I regret that I ever agreed to allow you to learn."

Audra's face crumpled as he set her gently on her feet. "But, Mother…"

"If this is to be a sport, Audra, you must follow the rules," Thea insisted. "Only then can you all be safe."

Audra hung her head. "I'm sorry."

Roth felt her pain, but he still couldn't understand why she'd felt the need to attack her brother.

Thea wasn't about to give any quarter. "I am not the one to whom you should apologize," she told the girl.

Audra glanced up at her brother from under her lashes. "I'm sorry, Shaw. I should have waited until you were ready. But I still think I can take you."

"Audra!" Thea cried.

Roth moved back between the two children and glanced from one to the other. "Pugilism has two purposes: as a sport and as a method of defense. Is there a reason you feel you must defend yourself against your brother, Audra?"

Thea looked at him askance. He shook his head in a silent plea for her to let Audra answer.

Audra kept her little head high. "Yes. Shaw's a bully. He makes fun of me and James."

He couldn't argue with her there. Thea's face fell, as if she hurt for her youngest two.

Roth looked to Shaw. "How do you answer your sister?"

Shaw raised his chin, though it had to be smarting. "If

I have behaved badly toward James or Audra, I apologize. And I will do my best not to treat them so in the future on one condition."

"Shaw," his mother scolded.

Audra met him look for look. "What condition?"

"You show me how you knocked me down."

Audra frowned. "Do you promise?"

Shaw nodded. "I promise."

Audra beamed. "Then I would be happy to show you what I did."

James stepped closer to them. "I should like to learn too."

"You can all learn," Roth assured them. "So long as your mother approves."

They looked to Thea. For some reason, her face was tight.

"So long as you are careful," she said. "Roth, when you have finished instructing the children, I'd like a word."

She swept out.

"You're in trouble," James said.

Roth had no idea what he had done, but he could only concur with James's assessment.

Her children were attacking each other. Thea caught her hands plucking at the flounces on her collar and forced them down to her sides as she hurried for the stairs. Was this the consequence of having a former military man as a tutor? Had she made yet another error in judgment by marrying Roth?

Everything had seemed to be going so well. Oh, there'd been the bump with Vernon, but that wasn't unusual. And her neighbors had been judgmental, but she'd expected that might happen. She had been prepared to weather the scandal of her unusual marriage. She'd wed Roth to protect her children, after all, yet her children did not seem very protected.

Only she had no recourse from that decision. A marriage could not be annulled from lack of consummation, and the only way to obtain a divorce was a full trial in the House of Lords. She shuddered just thinking about it.

He'd seemed so logical, so even-handed. It was clear James and Audra adored him, and even Shaw seemed to be yielding to his authority. But if they came to blows because of him, what could she make of it?

She took refuge at her desk in the library, sorting papers, preparing quills, and trying to find peace through purpose. But still her concerns nagged at her. When he came to find her a while later, she had her thoughts and arguments laid out on the cross-hatched papers in front of her.

"Nurse Waters is reading to the children," he said, coming to stand in front of her desk like one of her staff giving a report. "What did you wish to speak about, Thea?"

She stacked her papers neatly together and started with the first issue on her list. "For one thing, I believe I have been too lax in allowing you to set your own approach to their education. In future, you will discuss all lessons with me before giving them."

He said nothing. He just waited. Quietly. Patiently.

It didn't help her agitation.

"For another," she continued, glancing down at her notes, "I think this deference to me in front of the children is not conducive to their understanding of Society's conventions."

He cocked his head. "So, you want me to get approval before I do anything, but not ask for that approval in front of them."

And just like that, his logic knocked down all her pretensions. She dropped the papers and threw up her hands. "I sound completely contradictory! Forgive me, Roth. Sometimes I don't know my own mind."

He came to sit on the chair in front of her desk. "Everyone has moments when they wonder about choices they have made. Your choices carry more weight, so it isn't surprising you would wonder more. Yet, you were trained to be the countess, to manage lands, tenants, and staff. What makes you question that training?"

She met his gaze. There was no judgment, only concern.

"I'm not sure," she replied. "Perhaps I merely lack sufficient practice. Father always made the decisions, then explained them to me afterward. When I had to begin making decisions on my own, Thomas was there to advise and correct."

He frowned. "Why did your husband correct? Were you in error?"

Oh, so many times! But she did not like admitting that in front of him. She forced a laugh. "No one is infallible, Roth."

"No one is infallible," he agreed. "But some are better than others at making good choices. I would have thought you to be one of them."

"You are too kind." She leaned back in the chair. "The truth is, I may make decisions, but I always wonder if I chose rightly. So much depends on me."

"So much depends on you and those you have elected to represent you," he said. "If you hire the right people, your work should be easier."

"So it would seem," she allowed. "But then I've merely transferred the concern from the decision to the person making the decision."

"Do you trust me to care for your children?" he asked.

"Yes, but…"

He shook his head. "There is no but, Thea. Either you trust me or you do not. Have I done anything to make you doubt me?"

"No," she said. "Although this boxing…"

"You approved of Audra learning."

"I did. But that is the perfect illustration. I approved. I trusted you to undertake the instruction. Audra struck Shaw."

"And was Shaw irreparably damaged?"

She tsked. "No, of course not."

"Was his consequence so wounded he will lose confidence?"

She knew her oldest. "Not likely."

"Then what harm did it cause?" he asked, spreading his hands. "Audra is correct. Shaw bullies his sister and brother. If this makes him think twice about that, her striking him was a good thing."

"Striking someone is never a good thing," she said, but the primness in her voice nearly made her cringe. "The children should know that they can work out their differences by speaking to each other."

"Audra and James have tried speaking with Shaw," he pointed out. "He did not listen."

Thea made a face. "So he deserves to be struck?"

"No," he said. "They deserve the right to find another way to gain his attention. They appear to have done so."

She blew out a breath. "You will watch them?"

"Always."

How could she question such sincerity? "Then I suppose it's all right. And you don't have to ask me about the subjects you will teach."

"I would ask you in any event," he acknowledged. "You are their mother. You have every right and responsibility to be involved in their education."

She shoved her papers away from her. "You cannot know how good it is to hear you say that, Roth. Thomas seemed certain my judgment was suspect when it came to Shaw and James, and Westerbrook has been in full agreement. A mother tends to coddle her sons, you see."

"A mother wants the best for all her children," he replied. "That fact requires no correction." He rose. "Now, the children and I were planning to go onto the estate tomorrow and find a Christmas tree. Normally, I would wait until Christmas Eve, but this is a new custom here. I thought we might need more time to make the proper arrangements. Will you come with us?"

At least that was one area in which she had complete confidence, the plants that grew on her estate. Yes, even here, counsel was necessary. "We should confer with Mr. Price and Mr. Wilson first. They are our groundskeeper and head gardener."

He frowned. "You own all the land. I thought we'd merely hike into the closest woodland and find a suitable tree."

"We have no woodland that is not carefully designed and tended, sir," she informed him with a smile. "This is England, not the mountains of Batavaria."

Ah, that smile. It curved his lips and warmed her heart.

"Perhaps you would be so good as to send for them, then," he suggested.

She rang for Felden, who sent a footman. Roth returned to his seat and put his hands on his knees. She had seen him take the position before. Though his body was still, he looked like a panther, poised and ready to chase prey.

"There is no attack planned, to my knowledge," she said.

He raised a dark brow. "Enemies generally don't announce themselves. Best to be prepared."

She chuckled. "Is that how you guarded your king?"

She had the satisfaction of watching him relax, long legs stretching out in front of him.

"He should not have needed such guarding," he said. "He is much beloved. The difficulty arose after the war ended."

"Something about a lost kingdom?" Thea remembered.

He nodded. "When we defeated Napoleon, the Great Powers met and discussed how to divide the lands he had stolen. He had never fully conquered Batavaria, so we had no fear that it would not be returned to us. Instead, the Great Powers awarded it to our neighbor, Württemberg. That king had originally pledged himself to Napoleon but had been persuaded to take the side of the Allies in promise for new territory. Our territory."

"Well, how unfair," Thea said. "I hope your king protested."

Now he chuckled. "King Frederick is not one to go down quietly. He is called the Lion of the Alps for good reason. But, despite his roars, he and his sons were exiled. The Imperial Guard went with him, first to Italy, where various noblemen granted us asylum, then to the German states. But the King of Württemberg was not satisfied with merely ousting us. He feared we would return for what was ours. So, he sent assassins."

She shivered. "How horrid! Obviously, you prevailed."

"We subdued nearly a dozen over the years, but, thanks to Lord Belfort, Lord Ashforde, and the Duke of Wey, your king sided with ours, and King Frederick is returned to his home."

She offered him a commiserating smile. "It must have been difficult, watching over your shoulder, always expecting another blow."

He shrugged. "We were trained for such things."

"And you can put it behind you now?"

He looked down at his hands. "Not as easily as I had hoped."

She could imagine.

"Mr. Price and Mr. Wilson, your ladyship," Felden said from the doorway.

The two men came into the room. Mr. Price was as thin as a willow, with flyaway blond hair already mussed from pulling off his hat in deference. Mr. Wilson was built more like an oak barrel, wide in the middle and blunt on both ends. His bald dome gleamed in the candlelight.

"Gentlemen," Thea greeted them. "My husband tells me we must have a Christmas tree."

They frowned.

"A Christmas tree?" Mr. Wilson asked, glancing at Felden as if for confirmation.

Roth rose to address them, towering over both, and Mr. Price blinked so quickly she wondered his eyes did not tear up.

"A fir, pine, or spruce," Roth told them. "Six or seven feet tall. Well formed, not too thickly branched so as to leave room for decorations."

Mr. Wilson's face was a study in confusion. "What sort of decorations?"

"Small paper stars, ribbon, and the like," Roth told him.

"Won't the paper just wilt in the rain?" Mr. Price asked.

"We will be cutting the tree down and bringing it into the house," Roth explained.

They both stared at him.

Mr. Price recovered first. "Your ladyship, I must protest. The plantings were authorized by your father. They are most harmonious. To pluck out a tree..." He clutched his chest as if Roth had asked for his firstborn.

"If I may," Mr. Wilson interjected. "There is a copse of Norway spruce along the southern edge of the home farm. I've noticed they're starting to crowd each other. Taking one of them shouldn't hurt."

Mr. Price gazed at Thea hopefully.

She looked to her new husband. "Would a Norway spruce do, Roth?"

He nodded slowly. "That may be sufficient. Tomorrow, we will bundle the children against the cold and find out."

Roth caught himself smiling as he and Nurse Waters accompanied the children to their rooms that evening. He had appreciated the skills and knowledge of the other Imperial Guards. He, Huber, Keller, and Tanner had become friends over the years. Tanner in particular liked to tease him about his more serious nature.

Thea seemed to appreciate his thoughts, his opinions, regardless of how somber. She invited sharing. They would do well together.

"Can't I come too?" Audra begged as they reached the top of the stairs.

"You have your own bedchamber, Lady Audra," Waters scolded, seizing the girl's hand as if she'd never let go. "You do not need to sleep in your brothers' chambers."

"They aren't going to sleep," Audra complained, but she allowed herself to be led away.

"I'm glad you're more sensible about all this," James told Roth with a glance at the nurse's retreating back.

"You'll have to deal with Dumart again," Shaw pointed out.

But the valet merely bowed and left when Roth requested the boys' presence. Perhaps there was something to be said for being the lord of the manor.

"You could invite your mother too," Roth said as they consulted their search plan again in the schoolroom. Nearly three-quarters of the rooms had been crossed off, and the ones remaining were less likely to have hiding places.

"Mother's too busy," Shaw said, straightening.

"If we all help her, she might not be," Roth replied.

"What could we do?" James asked with a frown.

"You could look for problems around the castle," Roth suggested. "If you bring them to me, we could resolve at least some of them without troubling your mother."

James nodded eagerly.

"And Shaw," Roth continued, "I know she would appreciate your interest in how the estates are run."

"I would be delighted to learn more," he said with his usual lordly manner, "after we find the treasure." He turned for the door. "The library tonight. Mother should be finished with it by now."

She wasn't.

CHAPTER FIFTEEN

THEA SAT, NECK bent over a stack of papers on her desk. He could only wish she had asked his help with them, but he had no doubt she had earned a break. The boys paused in the doorway, and James looked to Roth. He nudged them forward.

The movement brought her head up, and she smiled. "Well, what a surprise. Why are you still up?"

"We need to search the premises," Roth told her. "I suggest you leave us to it."

Her brows rose as she did. "Rather high-handed of you, sir."

Now Shaw looked to him too.

Roth went to take her hand. "Allow me to escort you."

She didn't protest until they were in the darkened corridor. "What are you doing, Roth?"

"Giving you a moment to breathe and the boys something of their own," he explained. "Every new recruit struggles to find his place, but he has weapons and perhaps a horse that are all his. Your children are struggling to find their place. They want to be of service to you. Let them."

She opened her mouth, and he heard it—footsteps down by her suite. He put a finger to her lips, then turned her to face that direction in time to catch of flash of blue light over her shoulder.

"What is that?" she whispered.

"I don't know," he murmured back. "But I intend to find out. Stay here."

She caught his arm as he passed her. "I'm coming too. This is my home."

No time to argue. He nodded, and the two of them set out, but they had only reached the opening to the main corridor when a figure stepped out of it.

Roth drew up short, putting himself protectively in front of her.

Hartshorn raised his lamp, the light leaving shadows under his dark eyes. "Your ladyship, sir. Is something wrong?"

Roth tipped his chin down the wing's corridor. "We heard someone. Check Lady Alldene's room and mine and report back to us in the library."

"Right away, sir." He strode off.

"Could it have been a trick of the light?" Thea reasoned. "The moon reflected off a mirror, perhaps?"

"Perhaps," Roth said, hand on her elbow. "But I would prefer to know."

They returned to the library to find that the boys had finished.

"Nothing," James said dispiritedly.

Thea put an arm about her son's shoulders. "Are you certain? I always wondered why our forebears carved so much of the castle with flowers. Perhaps one hides a secret."

That set Shaw and James to roaming the room again, pressing at this carving and that.

"Do you know this to be a fact?" Roth murmured to her as they waited.

"There is a secret compartment in the head of the earl's bed," she whispered back. "Father showed it to me before the room became mine. I never found another, but that doesn't mean there are none."

Roth nodded. "It will give them a purpose."

Hartshorn returned then to inform them that he had located nothing of interest in any of the rooms along the wing.

"Then you heard the footsteps too, Mother?" James asked as Roth and Thea accompanied them back to their bedchambers after the library paneling had failed to yield any secrets.

"I didn't actually hear anything out of the ordinary," she admitted. "But I did see an odd light. There's likely a logical explanation for it."

James sighed.

Roth felt his frustration. If the footsteps they'd heard had not belonged to Hartshorn, who had been the footman on duty, then someone else was in the castle.

Could Westerbrook's spy be among them even now?

Thea made sure both her sons were tucked into bed before exiting the schoolroom wing. Her heart started beating faster when she spotted Roth waiting by the stairs.

"An escort," she teased, joining him. "How gallant."

"I would like the staff to search the castle," he said, turning to allow her access to the stairs.

"You want the staff to help the children find the treasure?" she asked as they started down for the chamber story. Felden must have decided to leave lamps burning on the stairs at least. "I thought you said it was important for the children to find it themselves."

"It is," he replied as they made the first turn. "I want the castle searched for whoever flashed that blue light."

She was glad he'd said who and not what. James needed no help believing in ghosts, and neither did some of her staff.

"You truly think there's someone hiding in the castle?" she asked as they reached the chamber story.

He lay his hand on the newel post as if to protect even it. "I want to eliminate that possibility. Would you like me to check your room now in case Hartshorn missed something?"

The light had flashed from that direction, but the thought of Roth in her bedchamber was far more disconcerting. "No, thank you. Martin should be waiting for me. Speak to Felden in the morning about your search, and keep me apprised of the results."

He inclined his head. "As you wish. Good night, Thea. Sleep well."

Between flashing lights and the door between their rooms, she was surprised she slept at all. As it was, she rose later than usual and went to the breakfast room to find Roth already in residence. After the first day, Mrs. Naughton had made sure to send up additional sustenance, and the sideboard groaned with eggs, bacon, toast, three kinds of scones, coffee, tea, and melted chocolate.

"Nothing," he said as she selected her usual toast and cup of chocolate.

"Nothing?" Thea asked as she took her seat. "You've already searched?"

"First thing this morning. Everything was in order." She felt his sigh.

"Then it was a flash of moonlight," she said, applying butter to her toast, "as I had thought."

"Perhaps."

Could that look get any darker? Thea set down her knife. "Not every matter involves death and destruction, Roth. There is such a thing as a benign disturbance."

He nodded to the footman to take his plate. "What sort of disturbance could be considered benign?"

"An improvement in the weather," she suggested, turning to the raspberry preserves. "Some disturbances might even be considered to the good. A new baby, for example."

"Our marriage," he added.

Thea smiled. "Yes. I would certainly call that a disturbance to the good."

"I hope you will always consider it such." He rose. "And I hope Christmas turns out that way as well. When you are ready, we will go in search of our tree."

He could not be satisfied by Felden's report. He and Thea had not imagined that light. But, at the moment, he had other matters to attend to. Bringing in the Christmas tree.

In Batavaria, he would have walked out into the forest, pushing through brush and thicket. Thea had called for the carriage, which took them down to the home farm. They then trooped out across the fields, frozen stubble crunching under their boots and breaths puffing out clouds in the cold, to where a cluster of tall Norwegian spruce grew at the edge of the estate. At least their tangy scent reminded Roth of home.

Only Batavaria was no longer home.

He also didn't have the option of choosing his own tree.

"This one, good sir?" Mr. Price warbled, gloved hand brushing the blue-green needles of a tall, stately specimen.

"I had thought this one," Mr. Wilson said with a nod to a fatter fellow.

Audra, who had been holding her mother's hand, looked to Roth. "What do you think?"

Thea was watching him as well. She'd worn a thick wool cloak with ermine edging the hood. Her blue eyes were bright with anticipation. He felt it too, and he knew it wasn't just from Christmas. Even with their misadventure last night, something was growing between them. Something he could not name for fear of it becoming one of James's phantoms.

"That," he said with a nod toward the one Mr. Price had offered, and the slender fellow puffed himself up with obvious pride.

Roth held out his hand. "The ax?"

Price and Wilson exchanged glances, then Wilson nodded to an associate who had joined them. "We'll see it chopped down and brought to the castle, sir."

He had thought to chop down the tree himself and help carry it to the castle, but apparently that was beneath the dignity of the lord of the manor.

"Thank you, gentlemen," Thea said for them all. "We will await it eagerly." She shepherded the children back to the coach.

Mr. Wilson took a step closer to Roth before he could follow. "And what shall we do with it when we arrive at the castle, sir?" He still sounded sincerely confused by the whole project.

"You will find a large pot awaiting you in the withdrawing room the countess favors on the ground floor," Roth told him. "Felden can direct you to it. Set the tree upright in the pot. You may need to brace it with stones to keep it steady. We will manage the rest."

Wilson nodded and stepped back.

"Is that all?" James asked after Roth had joined them in the carriage. The boy rocked against Thea as the coach started back to the castle, and for a moment Roth envied him.

"That," he told them all, "is only the beginning. Now we decorate it."

Audra wiggled on the other side of her mother, who offered her a smile. "I already made paper stars."

"And very good stars at that," Roth agreed. "But we will need another for the top. Thea, could you find her some gold paper?"

She turned her smile on him, and the coach warmed. "I know just the thing."

He smiled back and had the pleasure of seeing her cheeks pink. "Then I will entrust that task to you, Audra," he managed.

She nodded, wide-eyed.

"And what task will you set me?" Thea asked.

Dozens of ideas popped into his head, none of which was appropriate to speak of in front of the children and none of which fully aligned with their agreement of a marriage of convenience.

"We will also need ribbon to twine through the branches," he said. "Would you have some?"

Her smile broadened.

He had to force himself to look at the boys next to him. "Besides Audra's stars, we could use other baubles and bangles to hang around the ribbon. James, Shaw, see what you can find. Anything bright and pretty will do."

The boys exchanged glances, then nodded their agreement as well.

Thea glanced between her sons. "Perhaps Mr. Felden could be of assistance there."

Felden was only too glad to help. Roth presented the plan to him while the footmen were helping them off with their coats and cloaks. The butler thumped his fist to his chest, and Roth had to hide his smile at the attempt at the Batavarian salute.

"Delighted to be of assistance, sir," Felden said. "Come along, lads."

The boys went off, the rest of the staff following.

Thea stepped closer. "I can tell you have a vision for this Christmas tree. I only hope we can do it justice."

She left with Audra before he could tell her she'd

already exceeded any dream of Christmas just by being who she was.

How long since he'd had a family Christmas? The king and his sons had always had a tree, and the guards had had their own in the guardroom at whatever castle they had been using at the time. The guards had been a family, but he had never stopped missing his first family. Unbidden, the memory flooded back, one from the few Christmases he'd had with his soldier father.

"And now the star, Papa!"

Being lifted in hands both strong and loving. Having the honor of placing the paper star high on the tree, like the star that had heralded the arrival of the Christ child. Then standing tall, his piping voice melding with his father's bass, as they sang about angels calling from on high.

His cheeks were wet. He dashed away the tears. There was no shame in them, but he didn't want the sadness. Not today, when he had a chance for so much more. He went to see how the others were faring.

He found Shaw and James with Felden in the small chamber off the dining room where the staff finished preparing everything for a meal service. Two walls were lined with shelving, the upper portion with glass fronts; the lower portion, below a long counter, filled with drawers and cupboards.

"But it's a bent spoon," Shaw was protesting, frowning down at the object in Felden's gloved hand.

"Which should drape over the branch rather nicely," Felden insisted.

"Indeed it should," Roth said. "And exactly the sort of thing we're seeking."

Felden beamed.

Shaw did not look convinced. "It's rubbish."

"It's a symbol," Roth explained. "A spoon signifies having sufficient food, which is a blessing."

"Precisely," Felden agreed. "What about a fat red apple? I think we have one or two that haven't wizened yet."

"Excellent choice," Roth said. "James, you and Felden keep looking. Shaw, come with me."

Shaw followed him from the room.

"I have in mind a few of those silver acorns we found when we were searching the storage room in the main tower," Roth said, striding for the entry hall.

"This is a very odd custom," Shaw mumbled, but he kept pace even though he had to stretch his legs.

The footman on duty fetched their coats once more, and they braved the chill of the courtyard and the ramparts. The storage room was below the guardroom. Roth thought it might once have housed weapons, but the space had long since been used to collect whatever weather-hardy items the castle did not need on a regular basis. Among them had been a box with assorted silver and brass finials that had likely decorated various pieces of furniture over the years. The custom had fallen out of fashion, but some industrious ancestor of Thea's had kept the things nonetheless.

But when they reached the storage room, they could not locate the box.

"I set it right here," Shaw protested, pointing to a small metal stand along one wall.

"Could one of the staff have moved them?" Roth asked, peering under some stone benches.

He glanced up to find the boy shrugging. "I don't keep track of the cleaning schedules. But I think these things have **been** here for ages." His face settled into a scowl. "It's that thief again."

Roth straightened. "What thief?"

Shaw moved closer, gaze turning up to his. "I heard two of the maids talking. Things are going missing. They said there was a thief in the castle."

A chill went through him. Could that be the source

of the footsteps, a thief? "Have they spoken with your mother about this?"

Shaw shrugged again, but he dropped his gaze. "I have no idea. I suppose they would go to Mrs. Willoughby or Felden first. That's what the staff generally do, isn't it?"

Very likely. He understood the concept of reporting to a superior. It was one the military and the Imperial Guard cherished. But Felden had said nothing to him and neither had Thea. Perhaps it was time he involved himself more directly in determining the source of those footsteps.

"But we were saving that for when you were out of mourning," Martin protested as Thea pulled a length of silvery blue ribbon from her dressing table drawer.

"We can likely still use it after Christmas is over," Thea reasoned. And if sap from the tree ruined it, the price would be a small one to see Roth smile. Truly, she didn't think there was a more magnificent sight in all the world.

Her hand froze, and she took a step back from the dressing table. "That should be sufficient, Martin. Thank you for your help."

Her maid sighed as Thea carried her finds out into the corridor, where she could let her hot cheeks cool. When had she become enamored of her husband's smile? She had offered him a marriage of convenience. He had given her little reason to suggest he wanted anything more. She wasn't sure *she* wanted anything more. Despite her assertion, it was still quite possible she could bear another child. Her first three lay-ins had gone well, but nothing said the fourth would be as easy. She hardly wanted Shaw to become earl at this young age!

She needed to recall her purpose in this arrangement— safeguarding her children. And perhaps giving them a childhood more carefree than her own, which meant throwing herself into these Christmas preparations.

Besides the blue ribbon, she'd found a nice length of lavender and a pretty pale green. A shame the more vivid colors washed her out, for surely the tree would look more festive with scarlet and amethyst. As it was, she was simply happy to be out of her mourning black.

She located Audra in the nursery, where Waters was helping her finish her work.

"Look, Mother," her daughter said, holding up the lopsided star.

"It's lovely, darling," Thea assured her. "Let's take our treasures back down to the withdrawing room and see how the boys are coming along."

James, Shaw, and Roth had already regrouped in the withdrawing room and were tucking bits and bobs about the spruce, which the footmen had erected in one corner, away from the hearth. Felden, who was doing his best to assist, smiled at her daughter and nodded to the box on the side table. "I took the liberty of bringing down your other decorations, Lady Audra."

Audra set the gold star carefully aside and went to join her brothers in decorating.

Roth moved in next to Thea. She held up the ribbons. "Will these do?"

"They are perfect," he assured her, and it was all she could do not to swish her skirts like Audra in pride.

Together, they wove the bright ribbons among the dusky needles, bumping into the children, talking, and laughing. Finally, all pieces had been put on, save one.

"And now the gold star?" Audra begged.

"Hang onto it," Roth advised. He put both hands on her daughter's waist and hefted her up. Her squeal turned into a giggle, and she wiggled as she placed the star against the highest point. Something warm wrapped itself around Thea's heart. Roth gave Audra a hug before gently placing her on the floor.

"It looks very nice," James said, surprise evident in his voice.

"A credible job," Shaw agreed with a nod.

"It's lovely," Thea said. Her hand clasped Roth's, and the warmth blossomed to spread through her.

As if he were just as affected by the touch, Roth cleared his throat. "And now we sing."

Thea smiled at him. "Do you think we sing the same songs at Christmas, sir?"

He glanced down at her, brow furrowing. "What Christmas songs do you enjoy?"

"I know, I know!" Audra cried, and she began singing. "On the first day of Christmas, my true love gave to me a partridge in a spruce tree." She pointed to an odd-shaped bird one of the boys must have found in their rambles.

"It's a partridge in a pear tree," Shaw corrected her.

"I think Audra has the right of it," Thea replied, and she took up the next verse. "On the second day of Christmas my true love gave to me two turtle doves and a partridge in a spruce tree."

James added his voice to hers and Audra's. "On the third day of Christmas my true love gave to me, three Batavarian hens, two turtle doves, and a partridge in a spruce tree."

Roth was smiling as Shaw began the fourth verse and her husband's deeper voice took up the chorus. For a moment, Thea just allowed herself to feel. Joy, happiness, gratitude.

Love?

CHAPTER SIXTEEN

THEY WENT ALL the way through the song, from golden rings to lords a-leaping, which Shaw changed to guards a-leaping. When the last notes faded away, Roth nodded. "I like this song."

James and Shaw grinned at each other before Thea's oldest son remembered he was above such things.

"Well done, all," she agreed. "Shaw, James, Audra, you will need to wash up before dinner. Felden, if you would escort them?"

"This way, my dears," their butler said with a magnanimous wave.

Thea drew in a breath. The very air was scented with evergreen and rosemary. From the kitchen wafted scents of orange and ginger. With wreaths on the windows and the mirror over the hearth, swags up the stairwell, and her kissing bough in the entry hall, the entire house was ready for Christmas.

"Thank you," she said as she and Roth followed the children.

He raised a brow. "What have I done?"

She waved to indicate everything. "You make this castle feel like a home again."

Pink flashed in those chiseled cheeks. "If I have done that, then I am very pleased."

"There is no if, sir. Take the compliment."

He chuckled. "Very well. You are most welcome." He

sobered and drew her to a stop. "And I hate to interject trouble, but Shaw told me something you should know."

She sighed. "Oh, now what?"

Roth took a step closer. "Has Felden mentioned thefts to you?"

"Thefts?" Thea shook her head. "No. What sorts of thefts?"

"That part was not clear. But Shaw seemed to think things were going missing in the castle. I could only wonder about our ghost. Would you like me to look into the matter further?"

How nice to have someone else step up to help. "Yes, please. Let me know what you discover."

He inclined his head. "I am at your disposal, Thea." He offered her his arm, and she placed her hand on it. They strolled down the corridor and into the entry hall like a happily married couple.

And it struck her that she had never truly been a part of a happily married couple. Thomas had been her friend and helpmate. They had been comfortable together. This? This felt as if it could become more.

"I see you have been busy," he said as they came to a stop in the middle of the hall. A merry fire burned in the grate, and someone had draped a swag of evergreen about the neck of the suit of armor, as if the knight had decided to wear a scarf.

She smiled. "Audra and I had fun creating the decorations. So did Mrs. Willoughby and Waters, it seems."

"And that?" He tipped his chin toward the ceiling.

She glanced up. They were standing under the kissing bough. It hung there, so innocent.

So compelling.

She swallowed as she dropped her gaze to his. "Do you know what that is?"

"I am aware of the English custom. It is a kissing bough, is it not?"

She nodded.

"You have been kind to follow my customs," he murmured. "I should honor yours as well."

Slowly, softly, he lowered his head and kissed her.

The gentle pressure spread warmth through her, raising hopes, dreams, she had thought dead and buried.

He stole her breath.

And, she feared, her heart.

What had he done?

He hadn't intended to kiss her. He had no right. But the kissing ball, her sweet gaze, and the warmth of the moment had encouraged him to touch his lips to hers.

And now he could never forget that touch.

One kiss had opened the gates for hope, for home.

For love?

He drew back, and she stared at him. One hand came up to brush her lips, eyes shining. There was nothing for it. He pulled her close once more.

Footsteps sounded on the stairs, as loud as thunder. He broke away from Thea, and she scrambled back from him as if they had been caught stealing the silver. Audra, James, and Shaw spilled out into the entry hall. The two youngest children kept going toward the dining room. Shaw stopped, glanced up at the kissing ball, and then back at them. Roth couldn't know what thoughts were swirling behind those blue eyes.

"Are you coming to dinner?" he finally asked.

Thea's laugh sounded brittle. "Dinner. Of course." She fell into step beside her son without another look at Roth.

But hope, once freed, was reluctant to return to its

confines. All through dinner, his gaze sought hers, watching as her lashes fluttered, as she bit her lip and dropped her gaze to her mutton, as she smiled at the children and seemed to be having a difficult time attending to the conversation.

He certainly was. All he could think about was that kiss. She hadn't refused him. Some might say she had been as eager as he for the second. Could she have feelings for him?

Would she countenance him having feelings for her?

He managed to put himself beside her as they all started from the dining room. "We should talk."

Her smile was overly bright. "I believe you intended to speak to Felden about a matter first."

She didn't want to discuss the kiss. His spirits plummeted. "Of course." He dropped back and watched her walk away, skirts swaying. With a sigh, he went to seek the butler.

He located Felden in the entry hall, coming back from his own dinner, and Roth did his best not to glance up at the kissing ball or remember the feel of Thea in his arms.

"I heard a report of thefts in the castle," he told the butler. "Can you confirm or deny?"

Felden rubbed his chin with one hand. "I'm not sure I can do either. A few things have gone missing. I noticed one of Mr. Westerbrook's silver snuff boxes was not where it should have been when we prepared the master suite for you, and some of the staff have noted small items like candlesticks and vases disappearing. I haven't been able to determine whether they were merely misplaced or had another reason for going astray."

"But you are assured that nothing belonging to the countess or the children has been touched?" Roth pressed.

He drew himself up. "No one would be so bold as to steal from Lady Alldene herself. She is much beloved."

The kissing bough taunted him. "So I understand. But there is the matter of those footsteps."

Felden went so far as to sigh. "Could they not be merely the settling of an old building in the cold?"

A settling with direction and movement, armed with a light that flashed blue? He had stayed in many castles over the years, some older than this one, and he had never experienced such things. But he couldn't do much more than he already had, short of patrolling the corridors himself every night. And that was not exactly the role of the lord of the manor.

"Then you have the matter in hand?" he asked the butler.

"I do, sir. You can trust me to protect the castle and all its occupants."

Protection had once been his job. He could not lay it down so easily. "Report to me if you discover anything else missing."

Felden inclined his head, and Roth went to join Thea and the children.

They spent the evening reading from an adventure novel the children found fascinating. He would have as well, had he not lived a few too many adventures in his life. Every time the hero dashed forward, sword drawn, he wanted to caution the man to think first, find his opponent's weakness before striking.

"One more chapter?" Audra begged when Thea closed the cover.

"Tomorrow," she promised her daughter with a smile.

Roth rose. "Then it is time for bed."

Thea surged to her feet. "Yes, yes, it is. Come, my dears. I'll see you up to your rooms."

"And will you tuck us in and sing us a lullaby?" Audra asked.

Shaw made a gagging sound.

"For those who enjoy such things," Thea said. She did not look his way as they left the room.

Thwarted, Roth returned to his bedchamber. The door to her suite no longer whispered. It shouted. But if she could avoid him, he could ignore it. Perhaps.

They were all heading to Rose Hill the next day for Lady Belfort's Christmas Eve party. Roth had hoped to catch Thea over breakfast, but he tarried in the room for an hour, and she never appeared.

"In her suite, preparing for your outing, sir," Felden replied when Roth finally inquired about her.

Even in the daylight, he hesitated to confront her in her bedchamber, so he waited in the entry hall. The children joined him first, so well bundled he wondered whether they would be able to enjoy the activities. Finally Thea appeared, gowned in embroidered blue wool with sturdy boots, an outfit she quickly had the footman cover in her cloak with the ermine-edged hood.

"Won't you be cold?" Audra asked him, eyeing his wool coat.

He smiled down at her as he accepted his greatcoat from Griggs. "I was raised in much colder weather than this. Your English winter is like a Batavarian spring."

She shivered.

Mr. Yancey, the coachman, had plenty of blankets and hot bricks in the coach to warm them, so the ride was accomplished in comfort, if not quiet.

"What are you looking forward to?" Thea asked the children as they came down off the castle mount.

"Snowball fights!" Audra cried, bouncing on the padded leather seat.

Thea's face softened. "Darling, it hasn't snowed."

"It hasn't snowed at the castle," Audra said, lower lip beginning to tremble. "Maybe it snowed at Rose Hill."

"It has been cold enough to freeze the pond there," Roth suggested. "You could skate."

She nodded, but she settled back in her seat with a sigh.

"I hope Lady Belfort will have gingerbread," James ventured.

"I imagine she will," Roth said. "Her cook told me it is one of Lord Belfort's favorites."

"And do we know whether he has returned?" Thea asked.

Finally, she glanced toward him. He did his best to smile in encouragement. "I have not heard, but I can only hope so for her ladyship's sake. They are devoted to each other."

She looked away, and some of the light left the coach. "What about you, Shaw?"

"A good conversation with a peer would not be unwelcome," he said loftily from beside Roth.

Roth lay a hand on the boy's shoulder. "Lord Thalston will have been invited."

James brightened. "That means Lord Peter will be there too!"

The two sons of the Duke of Wey, who were only a little older than the boys, were obviously favorites.

"And Lady Sophia," Thea said with a look to Audra, "Lord Kendall's daughter."

Audra made a face. "She acts like she hung the moon."

Thea raised her brows. "Wherever did you hear that expression?"

"Nurse Waters said it about Miss Latterly," she said. "I had to ask her what it meant. She said it meant someone who thinks too highly of herself."

Thea met his gaze again. "Perhaps I should speak with Nurse Waters."

Roth nodded. The woman should have known better than to gossip in front of the little girl.

"But Lady Sophia is a true lady," Shaw put in, and Roth was surprised to see his face reddening. "You would be wise to watch and mimic her, Audra."

His sister scowled at him. "You promised not to bully!"

"That wasn't bullying," Shaw informed her. "It was merely a statement of opinion."

"Lady Sophia was at the Duchess of Wey's house party earlier this year," Roth said before the two could come to blows again. "She is a fine young lady, greatly to be admired."

Shaw nodded as if that were that.

"She probably doesn't know how to box," Audra muttered, little hands fisting.

"As her stepmother is the sister of the Beast of Birmingham, once the bare knuckles champion of all England," Roth said, "I wouldn't wager on that."

Audra perked up. "Then I would very much like to renew our acquaintance."

A short time later, they turned onto the long drive to Rose Hill. The trees on either side were bare and frosted white in places, and he saw immediately that he had been right about the pond, which was a glimmer of ice across the front of the square house. Wreaths hung from every window and on each of the double doors at the front. Already light spilled out to sparkle on the frosted shrubs.

Mr. Cowls, the butler, welcomed Roth into the entry hall as warmly as his starched consequence would allow. Here too, wreaths and evergreen swags draped everything from the paneled walls to the stairway leading to the chamber story. At least Lady Belfort's forebears had opted for polished wood instead of all the carved flowers at Alldene. Roth's gaze, however, was drawn to the kissing bough hanging from the chandelier. Thea was also looking up at it. She glanced his way and blushed.

"Thea, dear, so good to see you," Lady Belfort greeted her. The two exchanged fond smiles before her ladyship turned to Roth and the children. "And Roth, Lord Shaw, James, and Lady Audra. We are delighted to have you with us."

Roth was more pleased to see the man at her side. Julian, Lord Belfort, was as dapper as ever, his reddish-gold hair carefully combed, his beard and mustache well trimmed. But it seemed to Roth that more lines bracketed his eyes.

"Welcome home, my lord," Roth said with a bow. "How went your trip?"

"I can rightly say that your country is beautiful, Roth," he replied, "and your people are delighted to have their king back." He held out a hand, and Roth shook it.

"Then you had no trouble?" he asked as Thea, Lady Belfort, and the children chatted.

"It was nip and tuck for a while," Lord Belfort admitted. "But we managed to sort things out. I'm just glad to be home. King Frederick sends his regards."

Roth inclined his head. "He is kind to remember me."

"You and all the guards. He was surprised you didn't want to come with us."

"Batavaria is no longer home," Roth told him. "I do not miss it as much as I thought I would."

Lord Belfort's frank gaze lingered on Thea and the children. "I can imagine. Congratulations on your marriage, by the way."

"Thank you."

Others had entered, so Roth made way for them with their host and hostess. He had only spoken the truth. Sometime in the last month, his perspective had changed.

Thea had become home.

If he wanted a chance at a real marriage, he would have to tell her everything and hope she would still hold him in esteem.

This might have been Thea's first time at the Rose Hill Christmas Eve party, but it was clear others had long relished the tradition. Footmen waited at the edge of the sparkling pond to help guests on and off with skates, and His Grace, the Duke of Wey, glided past, arm in arm with his duchess, as Thea ventured out with Audra.

The lack of snow prevented the use of the sleigh, but Meredith had borrowed a wagon from her neighbors, the Garveys, decked the sturdy horses with sleigh bells, and placed cushions in the bed for her guests to take a ride along the River Road, where the Thames tumbled past, cold and silvery. She and James joined a pretty blonde who she had heard had been Meredith's former companion and her husband for one of the trips.

"You married Mr. Roth, I understand," she said with a fond smile that might have made Thea a little jealous if she hadn't seen the warm looks flashing between the couple. "I had the honor of tutoring him for a time."

"You tutored our tutor?" James blurted out before hastily lowering his gaze and begging everyone's pardon.

"No need," the young lady assured him. "And yes, I helped all the Imperial Guards understand what it means to behave as Englishmen, even my husband."

Her dark-haired husband smiled so broadly it lit his amber-colored eyes, and he bowed as best he could to Thea. "Finn Huber, at your service, Lady Alldene. It is a pleasure to meet the woman who captured Stephen Roth's heart. You must be very wise and very patient."

"She is," James said, and they all laughed.

But perhaps the best moment came when Fortune had approached Shaw as he was speaking with the sophisticated fourteen-year-old Lady Sophia in the

Great Hall. The cat rubbed herself against his boots, purr audible even against the other nearby conversations.

"Fortune approves of you," Lady Sophia said with a look Thea's oldest must appreciate. "You must be of very fine character indeed."

Cheeks reddening, Shaw unbent enough to pet the cat and murmur something into her grey ear.

Life was good.

Well, except for the fact that Thea was avoiding her husband.

It wasn't right. She knew that. He had done nothing for which he needed to apologize. But that kiss! Every time she passed through the entry hall with Lady Belfort's kissing bough, she remembered the feel of his arms around her, the insistence of his lips against hers. Every time he glanced her way, she'd relived the giddy feeling of being admired, treasured.

She wasn't a green girl on her first Season. She was the mother of three children! She knew the relationships between husband and wife. At least, she'd thought she'd known. Thomas's kisses had been warm, encouraging.

This one had been something else: stronger, more powerful, much like the man who had delivered it. She tingled at the thought.

Was it possible her father had been wrong about marrying for duty? Could a countess fall passionately in love with her own husband and he with her? Was she mad to even consider broaching the subject?

CHAPTER SEVENTEEN

THEA TOOK A moment to sit by the hearth in the Great Hall while a quartet played carols and some of Lady Belfort's neighbors sang along. The children had gone with Roth to the refreshment table that stretched all along the back wall. Something brushed her skirts.

Glancing down, she smiled at the grey tail, tall and proud, disappearing behind her chair. "No need to run. I'd be delighted to share."

Fortune stalked around her other side and considered her a moment, then jumped up into her lap. Thea ran her hand down the soft fur.

"Congratulating herself, is she?" Meredith mused, wandering closer. The aroma from her cup of spiced cider teased Thea's nose. "I think she is very pleased with herself that you and Mr. Roth are getting on so well."

Her face was growing hot again. She pivoted away from the hearth beside her, and Fortune jumped down to scurry off. "Does she always know? About husband and wives, I mean."

Meredith sank onto the chair next to hers. "She seems to sense happiness and unhappiness and how to turn the latter into the former."

Thea swallowed. "Even among those who marry for convenience?"

"Ah," Meredith said as if understanding more than Thea had intended. "Well, she matched Ivy with Kendall, and theirs was a marriage of convenience." She nodded across the room to where the marchioness and her husband were taking turns adding tidbits to each other's plate. A more besotted pair she was unlikely to find.

"I could wish for such happiness," Thea murmured.

Meredith's hand covered hers. "You have every chance. You simply have to decide to take it."

Thea blew out a breath. "Decisions are sometimes challenging for me."

Meredith squeezed her hand before withdrawing. "Surely not when the decision is this important. Now, I think something sweet is called for."

She'd already had her share of the gingerbread, marzipan, and sugarplums that graced the refreshment table, but perhaps another bite would not be remiss. Thea rose with her friend. But Meredith was right about another matter as well. The decision about Roth wasn't all that difficult.

If she wanted a real marriage, she must tell him.

So, she waited only until they had returned home and seen the children to bed before asking him to speak with her. She had no interest in the cavernous withdrawing room, and she certainly wasn't going to pass through the entry hall and its tempting kissing bough. So, she led him to her library and took a seat on the chair nearest the hearth.

A lamp had been lit on her desk, casting the room in a golden glow, but the hearth was cold. He bent to light the coals, graceful, powerful, at ease in his own capabilities. How could she not admire him?

"I have had trouble of late with decisions," she said. "I believe the correct term for my behavior is dithering. I do not want to be someone who dithers. So, I will say it outright." She squared her shoulders. "I am developing feelings for you that are not in keeping for our agreement."

He glanced back at her, the growing glow from the coals edging his cheeks in red. "You are upset with me?"

"No, no." Arg, could she do this any more badly? "I am falling in love with you, Roth. That was not the arrangement."

He rose, a tall shadow against the lamplight. "It was not, but I cannot regret it. I am already in love with you."

"Oh." All the air seemed to have left the room. Certainly it had left her lungs. She swallowed, but still no words came out as he sat on the chair closest to hers.

"Now are you angry with me?"

"No, never." She was chattering! She straightened her spine once more. "I am very glad we are of one accord. We simply need to decide what we intend to do about it."

"It is perhaps not so easy," he allowed, and she realized he was sitting as stiffly as she was. "There are things about me that you do not know. They might change how you feel about me."

"Oh?" she said when all she wanted to do was promise nothing he could say would change her feelings. But she was a countess after all. She had some ability to control herself. Usually.

"You see me as a gentleman," he said, "and I have tried hard to behave as one. But I was not always a soldier or an Imperial Guard."

"I know you worked in a silver mine," she said. "Humble beginnings are no reason for shame."

"Being a thief is."

She caught her breath. "A thief? Surely not."

He nodded. "Life was hard. I had been working for nearly ten years, with no hope for a different future, when I saw a chance for more. I stole the weekly pay bag for the mine, and, when someone challenged me as I was escaping, I struck him down."

She pressed her knuckles against her lips, unable to take her gaze from his. "You killed a man?"

"I have killed many men in battle," he said gently,

"but not that day. Still my actions were enough to see me convicted and sentenced to prison. When the king needed soldiers to fight Napoleon, he offered to pardon any who would serve. I agreed. Through my service, I was admitted to the military academy and then to the Imperial Guard."

She dropped her hand. "Then you are not that man anymore."

"No," he said. "But I ask your forgiveness for not telling you sooner. You might not have chosen me to teach your sons or share your home."

Thea shook her head. "You're wrong. You have no need for my forgiveness. You have paid for your crimes and sought to live a more honorable life."

"I have, Thea, I promise you." His gaze was haunted. "But not everyone agrees with your assessment. Once a thief, always a thief."

"Mother?"

She looked up to find Shaw standing in the doorway, glancing between them. His face was as white as his nightshirt. Concern forced her to her feet even as Roth rose as well.

"Shaw?" she asked. "Is something wrong?"

Still his gaze swung from one to the other, as if he could not reconcile the picture they made. "I couldn't fall asleep."

"I'll see what I can do," Roth told her. "I have given you much to consider. We can continue our conversation tomorrow."

She sank onto the chair as he escorted Shaw out. A conversation, he said. She had a feeling what was between them would never be satisfied by talking.

She cared about him, and she hadn't turned away when he'd told her about his past. Roth wasn't sure which surprised him more as he walked Shaw back up to the schoolroom wing. Was it possible they could build a true marriage together?

He shook himself. At the moment, he should give his attention to the lad beside him. In his long white nightshirt, his hair tousled from the bed, Shaw looked far younger than his ten years.

"After so exciting a day and with Christmas tomorrow, it is no wonder you found it hard to sleep," Roth ventured.

Shaw cast him a quick glance. "It wasn't the party. I was thinking we still had time to find the treasure, and then I heard footsteps."

Roth stopped on the landing. "Where?"

"Outside my door." The boy rubbed a hand up his arm. "I really thought it was all James's imagination. Many things worry him. You and Mother were just kind to humor him." He glanced at Roth. "But I heard them too, and, when I opened the door, no one was there."

"Did you see the blue light?" Roth asked.

Shaw nodded. "Down by the tutor's quarters. I came to find you."

"Very wise," Roth said. "That room is empty as far as I know. We'll look in it and the other rooms along the wing."

Shaw stayed close to Roth's side as they continued up the stairs to the top floor. This time, lamps had been left burning along the main corridor. Putting a finger to his lips, Roth looked toward James's bedchamber. Shaw's eyes widened as if he understood.

Roth eased open the door. Golden light trickled across the carpet and brushed the great bed. James's figure was a small lump under the covers, and Roth could hear the even cadence of his breath. Otherwise, the room seemed unoccupied.

He and Shaw checked the schoolroom next, but nothing appeared to have been disturbed. As he had suspected, the tutor's room looked just as it had when Felden had first shown it to him.

"Let's try the gentlemen's salon," Shaw said as Roth shut the door.

He was tempted to send Shaw to his room for his own safety but decided against it. The boy had a right to know who was in his home, and he would sleep better if they caught the miscreant. Besides, if there was trouble, Roth could protect him.

He led Shaw around the corner onto the main corridor, past the nursery, and looked through the door into the room where they practiced. It lay as they had left it, just like the schoolroom. He took a chance and opened the door to the nursery, but Audra was clearly asleep, as was Nurse Waters, who could be seen through the open door of her room off one corner, mouth open and snore rumbling out.

Roth shut the door and looked down the corridor. "The servants have rooms in the east wing, if memory serves."

"It wasn't a servant," Shaw insisted.

Roth had thought as much. The only family room left was the storage room that had been his bedchamber. He led Shaw to it and opened the door. Apparently Felden had yet to move most of the furnishings, for the bed, trunk, and washstand remained.

"Has anyone else been in this room?" he asked Shaw.

"We haven't," Shaw promised him. "There was no reason, with you downstairs with Mother."

Was there an edge to the boy's voice, or was his own conscience poking at him?

"Fetch the lamp from the corridor," Roth told him.

Shaw didn't argue, returning a few moments later. Roth took the lamp from him and held it high, further illuminating the cold room. He stalked to the trunk and threw open the lid.

A silver acorn glinted in the light.

Shaw bent to pick it up. "Is that where they went?"

"Someone moved it there," Roth said, lowering the lid. "But where are the others?"

Shaw sucked in a breath. "Then I was right. Someone was poking around where they shouldn't."

"Whether they should or should not have been here, we cannot know," Roth reasoned. "Felden may have been storing things here. It was a storeroom when I arrived. I will speak to him tonight. And I will ask him to put a footman on this wing until morning."

"Good," Shaw said as they came out of the room. He aimed another quick glance at Roth as he returned the lamp to its spot. "Thank you for believing me."

"You have never lied to me," Roth said as they started back across the corridor for the boy's room.

"You lied," Shaw said.

Roth stopped as the boy went into his bedchamber. "What?"

Shaw climbed into the bed and pulled the covers around him before answering. "You said you wouldn't try to become my father."

Tension sloughed off his shoulders. "I am not attempting to become your father. I know I can never take his place in your heart, nor should I. But I can be your friend, and your mother's."

"Maybe," Shaw said, then he covered a yawn with one hand. "Good night, Roth."

Thea a difficult time falling asleep that night. It wasn't the connecting door. She made sure to turn her back on it and shut her eyes tight. It was Roth's confession and his promise they would talk more tomorrow. Why hadn't he wanted to settle the matter tonight? Had she mistaken him?

No! He had said he was in love with her. Just thinking about the way he'd looked—tender, devoted—set her to trembling from head to toe.

Had any of her swains professed their love? They had said they adored her, that she was a pearl above price. They had extolled her beauty, her grace. Even Thomas had never claimed to love her. He had mentioned being fond of her, and she had been fond of him. She had considered them partners.

Yet her partnership with Roth felt different. He was at her side, a wall she could lean against. And though he might seek to understand her reasoning, he never questioned her decisions the way Thomas had.

In the quiet and dark, memories tiptoed closer, vying for her attention.

"I just found Price planting rosebushes along the drive," Thomas said, coming into the library where she had been working on their investment strategy for the quarter. "He assured me you had approved the idea, and I assured him he was mistaken."

"I thought they would look pretty come summer," Thea said.

He laughed. "Ah, Thea. Always an eye for beauty. Roses are generally tended by the lady of the house, and they require a great deal of tending, my dear. You simply don't have the time for it. Leave decisions about the castle to me."

She had wondered why their gardener couldn't do the tending instead, but she hadn't wanted to argue over such a little thing. But Thomas always seemed to have a reason to argue, gently, kindly. He'd even questioned her at Audra's christening.

"Audra?" He frowned down at the sleeping baby in her

arms, one of the few times since that her daughter had been still. "I'm sure we agreed on Thomasina."

Hand poised over the parish registry, Mr. Bloomsberg glanced between them.

"No, Audra," Thea insisted. "After my grandmother."

"Well, darling, if that pleases you," he'd replied with a shake of his head and a look to the minister that said she must be humored.

Had it always been that way? Now freed, the memories pummeled her. Thomas, questioning her judgment. Thomas, correcting her decisions so often that she'd begun to doubt them. Thomas, making his detestable cousin guardian of her sons, as if she wasn't a good mother.

Small wonder she struggled to believe in herself.

She threw back the covers and went to light a candle. Staring at herself in the dressing table mirror, she raised her chin.

"You are a countess. It is time you started behaving like one."

The woman who gazed back at her looked determined, courageous, fierce.

A woman who would not accept defeat, even in matters of love.

Christmas morning dawned bright and cold. Mist hovered over the moat as the carriage drew them across the drawbridge and down into the village for St. Pancras'. The bells were ringing, and dozens of villagers who had not attended midnight services were heading for the church as well. Thea walked with one hand holding Audra's and the other James's and Shaw just beyond. Roth followed them, a protective shadow. They had breakfasted with the children, so they had not had a private moment to renew their conversation from last night, though his look across the table had warmed her more than her cup of chocolate. She must not dwell on that. Today was about remembering the Gift given on Christmas and being grateful.

But when he put a hand to the small of her back to help her into the pew, she was certain she felt the touch all the way to her heart.

Mrs. Winfield and her husband were greeting friends as Thea, Roth, and the children came out of services. The lady hurried over to meet them.

"Happy Christmas, Lady Alldene!" she warbled. "And children." She glanced up at Roth, eyes inquisitive. "Sir."

Roth inclined his head.

Mrs. Latterly and her daughter scurried over as well. "Did you have that Noel tree you talked about?" the widow wanted to know. At her elbow, her daughter glanced between Thea and Roth.

"It's a Christmas tree," Shaw informed them, as if to protect Thea from censure.

"And I put the star on top," Audra added.

"Did you indeed? Well, how nice." Mrs. Winfield's gaze met Thea's. "I do hope I have a chance to view such a novelty."

This was her cue to invite them all to visit. "Perhaps after Boxing Day," she said. "We intend to leave it up that long, don't we, Stephen, dear?"

Roth blinked. The ladies tittered. He squared his shoulders. "It is customary to leave the tree up for the duration of the Twelve Days of Christmas. You may view it any time before Epiphany." He took Thea's elbow and directed her and the children to the carriage.

"Do you enjoy their company?" he asked as they started back for the castle.

Audra was looking out the window, and James seemed to have found a thread on his coat that required pulling, but Shaw was watching her.

"Not always," Thea admitted. "But they are the closest things to neighbors we have, and the House of Alldene has always extended its friendship to its neighbors. A little forbearance is not a bad thing, Roth."

"True," he allowed. "Should I meet their husbands?"

"Mr. Latterly has passed. Perhaps Squire Winfield. We can invite them to dinner in the new year."

Shaw directed his gaze out the window as well.

Christmas dinner was served early, a plump goose with all the trimmings and plum pudding for dessert. Then they adjourned to the withdrawing room and sang more carols around the Christmas tree.

Felden came to speak to her and Roth while the children were digging through the sheet music to see what other songs might amuse them.

"Two packages arrived, your ladyship," he murmured. "From London. One for Lord Shaw and one for Master James. I believe they are from Lord Westerbrook. What would you like me to do with them?"

"He sends presents to the boys only, not Audra?"

She could take great pleasure in Roth's growl.

"He hasn't sent anything in the past," Thea told him before turning to her butler. "Let me open them first, Felden, just to be certain there's no mischief involved."

CHAPTER EIGHTEEN

THEA AND ROTH stepped out of the room while their butler went to fetch the packages.

"I had hoped Westerbrook was out of our lives," he murmured, keeping his gaze on the children. Shaw was attempting to persuade James that a lead soldier battle was more in keeping with the day.

"So had I," Thea agreed. "But I suppose we won't be shed of him until we notify the Chancelry Court of our marriage. And even then, I owe him some duty as family."

"There is duty, and there is encouragement," Roth said. "I do not intend to give him the latter."

"Neither do I," Thea assured him.

Felden returned then and held out the packages. She and Roth each took one and peeled off the paper wrapping them.

Roth shook out the length of black material. "He sends them dressing gowns?"

Thea's hands were trembling as she tugged the wrapping back into place. "He sends them robes for school. He is informing us that he still intends to control us through the boys." She thrust the package at her butler. "Shaw and James will not be needing these. See them burned, Felden."

"With pleasure, your ladyship," he said, accepting Roth's package as well. He bowed and strutted down the corridor.

Roth put a hand on her shoulder. "We will not allow Westerbrook to win, Thea."

She drew in a breath. "I want to believe that." She straightened. "I *will* believe that. You asked me a while ago why I question my decisions. I realized last night that part of the problem lies with Thomas."

He cocked his head. "Your husband scolded you?"

"Not scolded," she said. "Just told me I was wrong at every turn, but with such charm that I rarely smarted under his correction. I'm not sure if he intended to cut me down to size from the start, or if it was just his way of making sure I knew I needed him. Either way, his actions made me wonder whether I was capable of making my own decisions. You don't treat me that way."

Something sparked in his dark eyes. "I will never treat you that way."

She caught his hand as he started to remove it and held on tight. "And I admire that about you, Roth. I admire a great many things about you."

His free hand came up to trail fire along her cheek. "Even after what I told you?"

"Yes. I hear the pain in your voice when you speak of those days. You regret it, deeply."

"I have paid for my crimes," he said. "I have fought and protected and served wherever I was needed."

She studied his face, the firm lines, the slash of black that was his brow. "Is that why you agreed to marry me? Are you still serving, Roth?"

"There is no shame in serving," he said, but his shoulders were stiffening.

"No shame at all," she agreed. "But a true marriage is a marriage of equals. Two people, becoming one."

He shook his head. "Thea, you have no equal."

"Within this castle and within my family, I should have," she said. "Give me that, Roth, and I will count myself fortunate indeed."

She wanted him to be her equal. She had no idea what she asked.

He had not been born the prince or earl she deserved. He would never have an enviable family line or estates that stretched across England. He was no investor who could lay an industrial empire at her feet. He had no jewels, paintings, or fine porcelain to offer.

"All I can do is try, Thea," he said. "For you."

Her smile said she had complete faith in him. He would have to find a similar faith.

"Mother!" Audra called from the withdrawing. "Come play Forfeits with us."

He must have made a face, for Thea laughed. "Do you not play Forfeits among the Imperial Guard?"

"What exactly am I expected to forfeit?" he asked.

"Your dignity, most likely," Thea warned him. She took his hand and tugged him back into the withdrawing room.

The children had gathered around one of the side tables, on which lay a top hat. His top hat. He looked to Audra, who grinned back at him, then James, who did the same, and Shaw, who was doing his best to look lordly again. Finally he looked to Felden along the wall. Their butler inclined his head as if acknowledging his part in this game.

"Ah," Thea said, going to sit on the sofa near the table. "And who will be the crier of the forfeits?"

"Shaw," Audra said with a sigh that proved she had hoped it would be her.

"We put tokens in for each of us," James explained. "If you successfully complete the forfeit, you may keep your token. If you do not, it must be returned to the hat, and you will have to try again."

Roth still wasn't sure what this game was all about, but the others were watching Shaw eagerly. The boy dipped a hand into the hat and came up with a tiny shell.

Audra bounced. "That's mine. What must I do to retrieve it, Shaw?"

Her brother's jaw worked as he likely reasoned through various choices. "You must pretend to be three different animals. First, a cat."

Audra plopped down on the carpet and tipped back her head. "Meow. Meow."

Roth hid a smile.

"Fortune doesn't make nearly as much noise," James complained.

"A pig," Shaw challenged.

She moved onto all fours and made snorting noises. Clever girl.

"A horse," Shaw ordered.

She frowned a moment, then climbed to her feet and began galloping around the room. Roth applauded, and she grinned.

"Horses neigh," James pointed out.

"I think we can safely say Audra has fulfilled her challenge," Thea said with a smile. She motioned to their daughter, who came back to join them. Shaw handed Audra the shell with a flourish, then plunged his hand back into the hat.

James stood on tiptoe, trying to see what was coming.

Shaw drew out a lead soldier.

"That's yours," James informed him, though Roth might have guessed as much. "I get to cry the forfeit."

Shaw's fist closed around the piece of metal. "Do your worst."

James screwed up his face. "You will not laugh for the next quarter hour."

Shaw snorted. "That's easy."

"It is?" His brother put a thumb in each ear and wiggled his fingers while sticking out his tongue.

Roth chuckled, but Shaw rolled his eyes.

As if determined to thwart him, Thea rose and held out her hands to Audra. "Dance with me, sweetheart."

Audra took her hands, and the two twirled around the room, until they both collapsed on the sofa, giggling.

Roth laughed, and Shaw's mouth twitched.

"That was a laugh!" James declared, pointing at him. "I heard it."

Shaw immediately sobered. "No, it wasn't."

"Nicely done, Shaw," Thea said. "Choose the next one while you wait out your turn."

He dipped in his hand again and drew out a tortoiseshell hair comb.

"Ah, that would be mine," Thea said. She waited expectantly.

"You," said Shaw, "must kiss the four corners of the room."

"You want your mother to kiss the paneling?" Roth asked, but Thea seemed to understand.

"Easily done, sir," she said. She popped up and headed for the Christmas tree.

James tugged on Roth's arm. "Come on."

He wasn't sure what the boy was about, but Audra took up her place in the corner to the right of the tree. James positioned Roth in the one opposite her before going to stand in the remaining corner.

Thea had discovered her daughter. "Clever miss." She bent and pecked Audra on the forehead. Turning, she headed for James and did the same for him. Then she turned and spotted Roth.

Her lashes fluttered.

His heart stuttered.

She approached slowly, carefully, as if afraid he might run. He could not have moved if he had tried.

Gaze turned up to his, she stood on tiptoe and brushed her lips across his cheek. He closed his eyes and let the warmth seep into him.

"Very good, Mother," Audra said, clapping her hands.

He opened his eyes to find Thea smiling at him.

"You laughed!" James pointed an accusing finger at his brother.

Shaw pressed a hand to his mouth as if to cover up his smile, but not before Audra joined in the cry. "You laughed! You lost your forfeit."

Shaw dropped his hand. "Well, you try to keep from laughing while they're *kissing!*"

All three children laughed at that.

Thea caught Roth's gaze. "Perhaps we should kiss more often if we can usher in such merriment."

"You will not find me arguing," Roth assured her.

Even she laughed at that.

They played other games until it was time to retire, then he joined Thea in seeing the children to their rooms. He left her singing a lullaby to Audra, the soft sound wrapping around his heart.

He lay on his bed a long time that night, watching as the fire died and the room descended into darkness. A husband could be expected to bring many things to a marriage—property, provision, protection. He could offer only the last, and he was, at best, superfluous, given the number of male retainers loyal to her. She needed nothing from him.

Nothing except his devotion.

That, he could give. He could be the man she could lean on, when she needed to lean. He could be the father to their children. He chuckled to himself. Had he once thought being a tutor beneath him? A father was tutor and mentor and disciplinarian and encourager and a host of other roles that might break some men. Being Thea's husband and Shaw, James, and Audra's father just might be the highest calling he could ever answer. He wasn't just protecting, he was building character, sowing for the future. What he did here could last for generations.

That he could give her.

He wasn't sure what time it was when he heard the door open and steps approaching his bed. Not the footman's or Felden's. He recognized those sounds now. These moved faster, more urgently. He caught the hand before it could touch his shoulder.

"What do you want?"

"It's me, Shaw." The voice trembled, but not in fright, he thought. "We found it, Roth. We found the treasure!"

He pushed himself up and lit the lamp. The boy's dressing gown was tightly cinched about his middle, as if he had girded himself for battle, and his eyes shone in the light.

"Where are James and Audra?" Roth asked, swinging his legs over the side of the bed.

"Telling Mother," Shaw explained. "It was in the gentlemen's salon, Roth. Mother was right about those flowers. Audra pressed one on the countess's throne, and a compartment popped open!"

Roth smiled. "You three couldn't wait until tomorrow to continue searching?"

He shook his head as Roth drew on his own dressing gown. "We wanted to give Mother a present for Christmas. It was easy to sneak out. Nurse Waters and the footman didn't even notice we'd left our rooms."

He would have to have words with the footman and the nurse. "Let's collect your mother, and you can show it to us."

Shoulders back and head high, the boy led him to the connecting door. Roth hesitated only a moment before following him through.

Thea was tying a satin dressing gown around her waist

while Audra hopped from foot to foot and James wrung his hands.

"It seems we have a treasure in the castle after all," she said with a smile his direction.

"So I hear," Roth said. "Shall we?"

Thea took the lamp, and the children led them up the stairs and down the corridor to the practice room. There, Shaw paused, hand on the latch.

"It's in a heavy box," he explained. "We couldn't move it. But Roth can."

He inclined his head.

Shaw pushed open the door, and they all piled into the room. The practice swords stood in their brackets; the mufflers hung from their hooks. The two thrones stood pressed against the wall, as if defending the room from interlopers, but the back of one was now a hollowed space.

An empty hollowed space.

Shaw rushed forward, washing white. "No! It's gone!"

James followed him, and they both peered into the cavity. "It can't be gone. It was right here!"

"Jewels and gold and silver, Mother," Audra insisted, pulling on Thea's hand to draw her closer to the chair. "Just like a dragon's hoard!"

"Someone stole it," James fretted. "While we were downstairs."

Shaw rounded on Roth, eyes blazing. "You!"

She had never seen her oldest son so angry. Crimson climbed in his cheeks, and he positively trembled with emotion.

"Shaw," she started, but he would not be gainsaid.

"You knew we were looking for the treasure," he

accused Roth. "You knew where we'd been and what rooms were left. You knew about the secret places."

"I did not steal the treasure," Roth said, face calm and gaze focused on her son.

"We found that acorn in your room," Shaw said.

Thea wasn't sure what he meant, but Roth replied with no hesitation. "The room has not been mine for more than a week."

Her son was unrepentant. "You were awake when I came to tell you."

Roth's gaze brushed hers for a moment. "I had a great deal on my mind."

"Because you needed money to impress Mother," Shaw said.

No! She would not believe it. Of all the men she'd met, he seemed to covet her wealth and position the least, if at all.

"Money would never be enough to make me your mother's equal," he said. "That is not what I can offer her or you. I can be her equal only in the devotion and care of this family."

He understood! She wanted to throw up her hands in thanksgiving.

"Shaw, I think you owe Roth an apology," she said, smiling at her husband.

Shaw rounded on her. "But he's a thief. I heard him tell you."

"I was a thief, once," Roth said, drawing Shaw's attention back to him. "I have paid for my crimes. I do not intend to ever return to that life. I did not take your treasure, Shaw, but I will do all I can to discover who did. I know what it meant to you."

Roth had been trying to tell her what the treasure meant to the children, but she still didn't understand. "Shaw?" she asked. "We have all we need. What could a few baubles possibly mean to you?"

Her son sucked in a breath, and she thought he was fighting tears. "Lord Westerbrook is constantly challenging you, Mother. I thought if we had more money, we could fight him off."

"Oh, Shaw." She went and gathered him close, his body stiff against hers. "Darling, it's not a lack of money that makes Lord Westerbrook challenge me. It's his need to control us. His consequence is too easily wounded, and he lashes out."

"Perhaps," Roth said. "But perhaps Shaw is right."

She looked up at him. So did Shaw. James and Audra were staring as well.

"Then you did steal the treasure?" Shaw asked, a catch in his voice.

"No, Shaw," Roth said. "But I begin to think I know who did. Will you allow me to help you?"

James raised his chin. "If he won't, I will."

Audra went to slip her hand into Roth's. "Me too."

Shaw pulled out of Thea's embrace. "I am willing to give you a chance, Father."

Roth's face softened. Thea had to hug her oldest son again before opening her arms and motioning her other children close. They huddled together for a moment, warmth and breath mingling. She glanced up.

"Well, Roth? What are you waiting for?"

He stepped to her side and wrapped his arms about them all. A fortress, a bulwark. Had she thought her castle enough to shelter them? What they had needed was a hero.

"So long as we stand together," he murmured, "no one can pull us apart."

"Let's go find our treasure," James said.

CHAPTER NINETEEN

ROTH GAZED DOWN at the four precious beings who had been given into his care. Four gazes looked back at him, trusting, confident that he would never fail them.

And he would never fail them.

"Audra, Thea," he said, "set up our command post in the library, Shaw, James, and I will gather our suspects."

Thea took her daughter's hand. "Come along, Audra. We have much to do."

Audra glanced at her brothers, then allowed her mother to lead her from the room.

"Who are we going to nab?" James asked, and for once he didn't sound worried about the matter.

"We will start by waking Felden," Roth said, ushering the boys from the room. "He will know who else we need to seek."

"Why?" asked Shaw as they started down the corridor for the stairs.

"Felden oversees the male staff," Roth replied.

"But you don't suspect him?" Shaw pressed.

"He has given me no reason to suspect him," Roth said. "Felden appears loyal to the family."

Shaw nodded as if he concurred.

The butler was already dressed when he opened the door to their knock. Shaw narrowed his eyes.

"Lord Shaw, Master James, sir," he said, glancing from one to the other. "Has something happened?"

"We need your help before you start your duties this morning," Roth told him. "Come with us to the library, and we will explain."

He shut his door and followed.

Around them, boards creaked, and footsteps sounded.

"Time for the staff to begin their work," Roth murmured to Shaw, who was walking beside him.

"So early?" Shaw asked.

James hastily hid a yawn.

"A great deal must be done for your life to be so easy," Roth said. "Have you never wondered who gathered the coal that feeds your fire? Who washes and presses the clothes you wear? Who sets the dinner table and ensures all the food is ready whenever you choose to eat it?"

Shaw glanced back at Felden. "Thank you, Felden."

"It has been my pleasure, Lord Shaw," Felden said. "All your staff are delighted to be of service to you and your entire family."

Roth did not challenge him on that. He was fairly sure at least one of the staff was not nearly so delighted.

They entered the library to find Thea behind the desk with Audra hopping from one woven flower to another on the carpet. She stopped when she spotted Felden and drew herself up.

"He didn't do it," she declared. "I like Felden."

The butler bowed to her. "And I very much like you, Lady Audra." He straightened. "But what is it that I haven't done?"

"The children's father told them that he had left them a treasure," Thea explained. "They found it tonight, but when they brought me and Roth back to view it, the treasure had disappeared. We are trying to determine what might have happened to it."

He glanced among them. "A treasure? What sort of treasure?"

"Jewels and gold," Audra supplied, waving her hands to indicate the size of the haul.

"Jewelry and small items," Shaw clarified. "In a chest about two feet by two feet, slipped into the countess's throne in the gentlemen's salon."

"We couldn't lift it out," James added.

"It sounds as if it would have required a man to lift," Roth put in. "Were all the doors secured last night?"

Felden threw back his shoulders, as if reporting to the general of the army. "They were, sir. I secured them myself. Whoever did this was inside the castle." His face was darkening with each word. "I will assemble the male staff of the house this minute." With another bow, he strode out.

"I find it hard to believe one of our staff would betray us this way," Thea said, hands braced on the desk. "Most have served for generations."

Roth went to lay a hand on her shoulder. "We will discover the truth."

The children settled on chairs around the desk, and, a few moments later, Felden brought in the male staff who served in the castle proper. There were five in all, including Felden: Peter, the lad who scrubbed the pots; Dumart, the boys' valet; Griggs, the footman, and Carter, the head footman. They all stood tall and straight, and more than one gaze was worried.

"Where is Hartshorn?" Roth asked.

"I couldn't locate him," Felden said, jaw tight.

Roth frowned. "Was he on duty last night?"

"No," Felden replied. "We generally rotate night duty, and he was on duty earlier in the week."

Griggs cleared his throat. "Begging your pardon, Mr. Felden, but he asked to take my turn last night so I could enjoy Christmas."

Carter started. "And me the night before." He looked to Thea, face reddening. "Forgive me, your ladyship. I should have noticed the pattern."

"So long as he gave good service, the pattern wouldn't have mattered," Thea assured him. "What's important now is that we find him and determine what he knows about the treasure the children found." She looked to the butler. "He is a more recent hire, if memory serves. Do you recall his credentials, Felden?"

"He had served in two other great houses, your ladyship, but his last employer refused to provide a reference."

"Why hire him, then?" Roth demanded.

"His last employer was Lord Westerbrook, sir. Mr. Westerbrook, the children's father, thought that if his cousin didn't appreciate the fellow, we might. A poke in his eye, as it were." He looked to Thea, face sagging. "It seems I must apologize as well, your ladyship. Our trust was ill placed. But I can vouch for the rest of my staff. No one would steal from you or the children. Or you, Mr. Roth," he hurried to add.

The other servants were all nodding earnestly.

Thea nodded too. "Very well, then. How do you suggest we proceed?"

Felden turned to his staff. "I shall speak with Mrs. Willoughby. She and Mrs. Naughton can search the kitchens and servants' quarters. Carter, Griggs, take the rest of the castle, from the living areas to the ramparts. Peter, I'm sending you down to the home farm. Tell Mr. Pennison to search the stables, barns, and outbuildings and to report anything he finds to me."

They fairly dashed from the room.

"I want to search too," Audra said, popping out of her seat. "Please, Mother?"

Thea glanced at Roth, and he shook his head. She nodded agreement. "It is entirely too dangerous, Audra," she told their daughter. "We will wait here. We try to surround ourselves with people we can trust. We must show them we trust them." She met Roth's gaze. "All of them."

He thought if his chest expanded any further he would be in danger of ripping out of his dressing gown. "All of them," he agreed.

In the end, they discovered that not only was Hartshorn missing, but so was one of the horses. And the coachmen and grooms had been apologetic that none had heard anything.

"He will be heading for London," Roth said. "I'll take two of the grooms. We can catch him."

Thea didn't like the thought of him harrying off after a villain, but she had to own there was no one more equipped to deal with one.

"Go," she said. "The children and I will await your return."

Even if waiting was hard.

She tried to keep busy. She returned the children to their bedchambers for dressing, then joined them in the schoolroom for breakfast. She tried to interest them in helping prepare the gifts for the Feast of St. Stephen, when the Alldene estate gave boxes to the poor. Nurse Waters bustled in and out, bringing clothing the children had outgrown and toys they no longer cared for to be included in boxes for the families with children.

Unfortunately, it was clear no one had the attention for it. Audra fidgeted in her seat, James kept glancing out the window, and even Shaw finally pushed away the box he had been filling with a sigh.

"Why don't you tell me about how you found this treasure?" Thea suggested while Nurse Waters went in search of a tea tray.

James brightened. "Shaw and Mr. Roth developed the plan," he told her eagerly. "We took portions of the castle in turn."

"Quartering, Mr. Roth called it," Shaw agreed. "He was very good about pointing us to places we might not have considered. I suppose that was because he was once a thief."

"You stop saying that!" Audra cried, hopping off the bench. She raised her fists.

"Sit down, Audra," Thea said. "You heard Roth admit to being a thief this morning. When he was a young man, he made a very poor choice indeed. He tried to steal money from his employer and was caught. He was severely punished. He endured the consequences and came out a stronger man for it. Since then, he has been a gentleman of honor and valor." She met her oldest son's gaze. "He has no reason to be ashamed. If he can put that time behind him, so must we."

"But he's a thief," Shaw started.

"He *was* a thief. Have you ever lied, Shaw?"

Her oldest son bit his lip as if to keep from replying.

"Sometimes," James said for him. "He doesn't like losing, so he pretends he hasn't."

"That's pretending, not lying," Shaw protested.

"In that case, are they not the same?" Thea asked him.

He looked at her defiantly for a moment, then dropped his gaze. "I suppose."

"So you are a liar."

He flinched.

Thea put her hand on his. "We all make mistakes, Shaw. They do not have to define our characters. What is important is that we learn from them and resolve not to make them a second time. And if we struggle, we can seek help from those who love us."

"Like you," Audra said, leaning against her.

Thea put her arm around her. "Like me, and Roth, and

your Heavenly Father. It says in the Bible that He has put our sins as far away as the east is from the west. That is a very far distance. We must do the same for Roth."

Somewhere downstairs, a door slammed, then they heard footsteps on the stairs.

Audra pulled away to dash to the door of the schoolroom. "They're back!"

A few moments later, Roth strode in. He hadn't even taken the time to shrug off his many-caped greatcoat, for it swirled around his legs as he came forward. Cheeks red from the cold, dark eyes bright, he set the chest he carried down on the worktable. It stood among the boxes as if daring her to open it.

"Shaw," he said. "Do the honors."

Thea rose and went to Roth's side, and he slipped his arm about her waist.

"You are safe?" she murmured.

"I'm fine," he replied. "But I'll explain later."

Relief and pride mingled.

Shaw had worked the latches and now threw back the lid. Candlelight winked on gold and silver, glowed in gems every color of the rainbow.

"See?" Audra said, pointing. "Jewels and gold and silver. Just like I said."

James picked up a fat gold star embedded with rubies. "Like the riches of King Arthur."

Thea's chest tightened.

Shaw looked to her. "Will it be enough, Mother?"

She went to hug him. "It's marvelous, Shaw. Thank you." She looked up to find Felden in the doorway. "Why don't you, James, and Audra have Felden show you where to put this to keep it secure until we can decide what to do with it?"

Felden came and lifted the chest in his arms. "This way, children."

They hurried out.

Roth was frowning at her. "You are not impressed."

She wrapped one arm about her middle, trying to hold in the emotions that threatened to spill out. The children had worked for this moment. They could have had no idea how much it hurt.

At least she could be honest with her husband.

"I recognize it, Roth," she told him. "Every piece. They had resided in various rooms and jewelry boxes, and I hadn't noticed them missing. I don't know why."

"You have been working hard," he started, but she shook her head.

"Don't you see? Hartshorn may have taken the chest, but he didn't fill it. He couldn't have known where half those pieces were stored or been able to open the chests that held them. Only one other person besides me had such access. Thomas told the children he had a treasure. Our treasure. He was stealing from me."

The realization of his betrayal sent waves through her, painful and hard. As if Roth sensed the darkness coming, he put both arms about her and held her close. Protecting her even from this.

"Perhaps he only meant to gather it as a game for the children," he murmured.

"I wish I could believe that," she said, aching. "But I can't. I only wonder what else might have gone missing over the years and I never noticed. As you've seen, it is a very large castle." She tried for a laugh, but it came out closer to a sob.

His arms tightened. "Do not blame yourself. You should know what Hartshorn told us when we caught up to him outside Weybridge."

She glanced up at him. "He confessed?"

"He could see he had no choice," Roth said, and the growl was back in his voice. She could imagine even their perfidious footman might have quailed before her husband's prowess.

"So he too had been stealing from the castle," she surmised.

"His were the footsteps we heard. The blue flash came from a hooded lantern. I have been told smugglers use them. Do you recall when Shaw mentioned the acorn we had found?"

She nodded. "I wondered at the time what he meant."

"While we were searching for the treasure, we came across a box of silver and brass finials shaped like acorns."

"I remember them," Thea marveled. "I never knew what had possessed Great-Aunt Ermintrude to commission them from the silversmith."

"They had disappeared by the time Shaw and I returned for them as possible decorations for the tree. Shaw suspected a thief, and he was right. Hartshorn was picking up whatever he could find, moving them from place to place, including the trunk in my former room, so no one would be the wiser. But he was not stealing from the castle or taking the chest for himself. He was doing it for Westerbrook."

Could the day get any worse? "What!"

"He admitted to being placed in the castle for that very purpose. He knew of the treasure."

She scrunched up her face. "Then had Thomas intended to offer all that to his cousin? Had he been supplying Westerbrook with things to sell?"

"We may never know," Roth replied, "but we can be thankful that he told the children in the end."

Thea gazed up at him. "Yes, but why steal to begin with? Did Westerbrook hold something over him? Was he merely trying to prove he was smarter than me? What else have I missed?"

"Little," he assured her, cradling her. "You manage this estate well, Thea. Your tenants and staff are happy and well cared for. Your children thrive. I do not like to speak ill of the dead, but it seems your first husband was not good for you."

"So I have concluded." She lay her head against his chest. "And I have also concluded that you are very good for me, Roth. You encourage me, you comfort me. You give me strength."

"And you have given me something I never thought to have: a true family."

She smiled against his waistcoat. "I'm so glad you feel that way."

His hand stroked her hair. "Marry me, Thea. Really marry me. Let me be the husband you deserve."

All of her trembled, and she glanced up again into his dear face. Those heavy brows were knit, his dark eyes dipping at the corners, as if everything in him hoped for her answer.

"Yes, Roth," she said. "That would please me very much."

He bent and kissed her. Warmth spread, and with it surety, peace, and a love she had never dreamed possible.

And she knew she would never hear the door between their rooms taunting her again.

CHAPTER TWENTY

TWO HEARTS BECOMING one, united in the love for each other and their family. It truly was the best Christmas he had ever had.

They spent the next two days of Christmas settling a number of issues. Thea didn't tell the children the origin of the treasure, but Roth helped her in gilding them to return the pieces to their original places in the castle. She also wrote to the Chancelry Court, informing them of her marriage to Roth and requesting formal removal of Westerbook as the boys' guardian.

"Perhaps Lord Belfort could appear on your behalf, if needed," Roth suggested. "He was a noted solicitor before King Frederick bestowed a title on him."

"An excellent idea," Thea agreed with a smile. "As usual."

Roth also made sure that the castle was appropriately protected. Lamps would now burn at certain locations each night, and Felden was interviewing local candidates to fill Hartshorn's position. All the staff were serving with renewed vigor, as if determined to honor their countess.

The outside staff joined him in searching the area, but they found no indications of any suspicious visitors to the inns or vagrants camping in the fields. Whoever Westerbrook had sent to watch the castle appeared to be gone. It seemed the viscount was out of their lives.

"But I won't believe it until I know he is finished," Thea

told him as she sat at the dressing table, brushing out her hair one night. Martin, her maid, seemed to delight in designing ever more complicated arrangements, which left her pale blond hair waving down her back by the end of the day.

Roth came up behind her and rubbed his hands across the shoulders of her lawn nightgown. He would not tell her he had woken twice the last two nights, simply to relish the fact that she shared his heart and his bed. He hoped he would never lose the awe and the joy of having her as his wife.

"I would prefer to deal with Westerbrook myself," he said as she swiveled to face him. "But every general deserves to accept surrender from her foe."

Thea nodded, setting her hair to glimmering in the candlelight. "Then we will go to London. Waters can watch the children."

He should not have been surprised to learn that the Alldene family had a townhouse leased in the metropolis. The small staff there were delighted to see Thea and meet him.

Lord Westerbrook, on the other hand, was not nearly so pleased.

He answered the door to his townhouse himself, then looked down his nose at her. "You've caught me at an inconvenient time. I was about to go out."

Roth didn't believe him. For one thing, he wore no coat, his form swathed in an emerald silk banyan. For another, no footman came hurrying to help him, and the walls of his pale green entry hall were suspiciously empty, as if all the paintings had been taken away for cleaning.

Or selling.

"We must speak," Roth told him, taking a step into the space and forcing him back as a result.

Westerbrook ignored him, focusing instead on Thea. "Well, of course I would make time for you, Thea."

"I'm glad to hear that," Thea said, settling her cloak about her. "I'll only take a moment. I wanted you to know that we are aware of your purpose in placing Hartshorn at the castle. The treasure has been located, he attempted to steal it for you along with some other items, and we caught him. He is awaiting trial. I am here to determine my options concerning you."

He glanced between them. "Hartshorn? Treasure? My dear, I have no idea…"

"He told us everything," Roth said. "You can stop pretending."

"Now, see here, sirrah," he said, taking another step back.

Thea held up a hand. "Spare us, Westerbrook. It seems you convinced Thomas to help you as well. I want to know why and how you intend to make restitution."

His face flamed. "Restitution? You are the one who should make restitution, madam. You led me on, raised my hopes for an alliance, only to throw me over for this, this, nobody!"

Roth stiffened, but Thea put a hand on his arm. "Do not strike him. You could be hung for it."

Westerbrook's smile was nasty. "Yes, do as your owner tells you, Roth."

Thea marched up to him, fisted her hand, and drove it into his jaw.

Roth blinked, then grinned, as Westerbrook stumbled back.

Thea followed. "You worm! Tell me the truth!"

He rubbed his jaw but was wise enough to stay out of her reach. Roth positioned himself to catch the miscreant should he attempt to escape out the door or up the stairs before Thea was satisfied.

"The truth?" Westerbrook sneered. "The truth is that you have more than you need. Thomas was kind enough to offer me a few pieces when times were tight. Times have become particularly tight in the last two years. He was supposed to help, but he died before he could do so. I tried to marry an heiress, but the Imperial Guards destroyed that chance."

"You destroyed that chance," Roth told him, widening his stance, "with your lies and manipulations."

His gaze turned feverish, and sweat glistened along his brow.

"Now I have nothing," he continued to Thea. "My creditors are knocking down my door, the Marquess of Norfall intends to bring me up on charges in the House of Lords for that business with the highwaymen this summer." He dropped his hand and took a step forward, searching her face as if for any sign of hope. "But you could still help me, Thea. We are family. What are a few thousand pounds in debt to you?"

Thea hesitated, glancing at Roth.

"You must do as you see fit," he told her. "We are to forgive those who ask it. But he did not ask, and there is no contrition in this one. He seeks only to use others."

She lowered her fists. "You're right. Westerbrook, it's time you faced the consequences. I will not shield you. Good day, sir."

They turned and walked out, and Roth wasn't surprised to hear the sound of something breaking behind them.

"Are you satisfied?" he asked Thea as they reached the carriage.

She glanced back at the house. "Satisfied? Yes. Lord Norfall will not allow him to wiggle off. Westerbrook's only choice is to run for the Continent and hope someone there might take him in. With his reputation in shreds, I doubt he will find one." She smiled at Roth. "But I think Audra isn't the only one you need to tutor in boxing. That stung!"

He took her hand and kissed it. "Next time, allow me the honor of defending you."

"I sincerely hope there will be no next time," she told him. "Let's go home."

Home. His home. His castle. His family. His wife.

His love. He never intended to leave.

Snow had been falling every day since they'd celebrated the New Year, but Meredith couldn't mind. It had given her and Julian an excuse to skate on the pond, to ride in the sleigh, and to chase each other about with snowballs.

"You still pack a punch," her husband had said, bending to retrieve the top hat she'd knocked flying. "To my heart and my wardrobe."

Meredith had laughed.

Oh, it was such a joy having him home again. She could not get enough of him. They had read together by the fire, walked hand in hand through the garden, and sat planning all the adventures they would have come spring.

Just as delightful was hearing from so many of her former clients and now friends. Jane and her duke, their daughter Larissa and Prince Otto Leopold, Jane's daughter Callie and Count Montalban, and her youngest Belle and her husband Owen had visited to welcome Julian home. Ivy and Kendall had come for the Christmas Eve party.

Patience and Sir Harry had written that they would visit in the spring, the winter being a difficult time to leave their island estate. Yvette and the earl were planning a soiree as soon as everyone returned to London. And Lydia, Worth, and their balloon had celebrated Christmas in the Hebrides.

Best of all, Meredith's Imperial Guards were all settled. Finn and Abigail had already made a home near Ivy's Villa Romanesque, Tanner and Julia would be leaving shortly for Egypt, and Mrs. Bee could not stop crowing about the marvelous Keller, who had married her oldest, Elspeth.

"We should invite the Alldene children to ride in the sleigh," she told Julian as they were sitting on the sofa in the withdrawing room, map spread on his lap. "Lady Audra so missed having snow around on Christmas Eve."

"Excellent idea," Julian said. "I must admit, I never thought to see Roth that happy. He and the countess positively glow."

She glanced to where Fortune was sitting on the sill, gazing out at the tufts of white drifting from the sky. "Fortune knew."

"Fortune always knows," Julian agreed.

As if quite satisfied with herself, her pet slipped down and padded over to the fire to curl up in the warmth. She smiled a little smile.

Dreaming of the future perhaps?

After all, another generation would one day look for their true loves. Who would match Lady Sophia? Lord Thalston? Lord Peter? And what of Lord Shaw, James, and Lady Audra?

Who else but a matchmaking cat could hunt true love?

THANK YOU FOR choosing Roth and Thea's story. I foresee a long, happy marriage for them, as well as the many other couples Fortune has matched over the years. If you missed the first book that started her matchmaking, look for *Never Doubt a Duke*.

Thea was a countess in her own right, which was unusual in Regency-era England, and so was an American inheriting an earldom. But that's just what happened in *Secrets and Sensibilities*, the first book in my Lady Emily Capers. That story also features an unusual treasure hunt and true love triumphing. Turn the page for a sneak peek.

SNEAK PEEK

REGINA SCOTT

CHAPTER ONE

Somerset, England
Spring, 1815

TO HANNAH ALEXANDER, people existed to be painted. Every wise old crone with a youthful twinkle in her eye, every stout gentleman of military bearing, every wide-eyed child with an endearing smile was a moment to be captured, recreated, embellished until the essence of them shone from her canvas for all to see. When she looked at those around her, she saw them frozen in a moment of perfection that illuminated their souls.

The farmer carrying a lamb home on his shoulders at sunset was the Good Shepherd. The girl flirting with the farmer's son outside church on Sunday was Aphrodite Taunting Hephaestus. The other teachers at the Barnsley School for Young Ladies gossiping about their charges' parents were The Three Witches from *Macbeth*. She thought she would be completely happy if only she could spend her days with her paint box and easel. And now, after years of dreaming, it had looked as if she might actually attain that happiness.

If only Miss Martingale hadn't insisted that she play chaperone first!

She should have known something was wrong when she'd received a summons to the headmistress's office.

Miss Martingale rarely addressed her subordinates unless something dire had happened. She could only hope that she had received no complaints against her teaching. She was aware that often she held control of her students by the slimmest of threads. She had never mastered the technique that so many of the other teachers used, namely of intimidating her pupils with her authority. At five feet, four inches, she did not tower over any of them.

To make matters worse, she was cursed with a clear-skinned, oval face; lustrous black hair; and large doe-like eyes that seemed to encourage condescending smiles rather than strict obedience. Her nose was short and pert, and her mouth tended far too often to smile. No, she had not been the most awe-inspiring of teachers, although her students did seem to learn their lessons, and more than one parent had complimented her on the girls' knowledge of art.

But it seemed that Miss Martingale had had other thoughts besides Hannah's performance on her mind.

"Priscilla Tate's aunt, Lady Brentfield, has graciously invited her niece and three friends for Easter holiday," she had proclaimed without roundaboutation before Hannah could so much as take a seat in the hard-backed chair in front of the desk that spanned the rear of the room. "I need you to chaperone."

Hannah had felt herself pale but had forced her dutiful smile to remain in place. She had always been able to reasonably discuss things with her employer. Surely Miss Martingale would not send her off simply to gratify the whims of four students.

"But I know nothing about deportment, Miss Martingale," she pointed out. "As you know, I was raised quietly in the country."

The large, dark-haired woman shrugged. "That is not important. Lady Brentfield can be counted on to enforce the social niceties. I need someone to chaperone them in the carriage on the ride to and from the estate, and Lady Brentfield has requested that we provide someone to assist her in monitoring the girls' activities when she is unavailable. A woman as busy as Lady Brentfield cannot be expected to watch them every minute."

So, Hannah was just supposed to be a nebulous body, at the beck and call of the socially astute Lady Brentfield. If the assignment had had any appeal before, it had none now. Hannah had only met Lady Brentfield a few times when the woman had visited the school, usually when she was fetching or returning Priscilla from some event.

But Hannah knew that her ladyship was a powerful influence. Miss Martingale gloated over any little kindness from the lady, and many of the teachers watched from the upper windows of the school to catch a glimpse of the latest styles her ladyship wore. Hannah could not imagine anything more mortifying than having to flutter about in the wake of this fashionable lady, her own lack of polish and ignorance of the upper class showing with each movement.

"Lady Brentfield will surely want someone with whom the girls are comfortable," she protested. "I barely know Priscilla and her friends."

"That is as it should be," Miss Martingale said with a regal incline of her broad head. "You know my policy that students and teachers should not fraternize. I have observed that you keep a distance from your students, which I applaud. I have also observed that they tend to ignore your commands. This trip will give you an opportunity to practice your disciplinary skills."

Practicing her disciplinary skills was the last thing on Hannah's mind, as was spending a week in close company with her students. The distance Miss Martingale had noted was there for a reason. She was trying to hide the fact that her students scared her not a little. The oldest was only three years her junior, after all. Her fear was easy to hide when she could focus on art, but she was sure they'd see right through her if she was forced to interact with them socially. Besides, spending a week at the Brentfield estate would delay her most recent commission.

"But I've just agreed to paint Squire Pentercast and his family," she explained to Miss Martingale, hoping the mention of the local landowner would inspire sufficient respect to allow her to remain at the school. "I'm sure one of the other teachers would love to go."

"Most have arranged to go home to their families," Miss Martingale replied, her considerable bulk beginning to tremble, most likely in indignation that Hannah continued to question her judgment. "And I cannot spare Miss Pritchett; she is needed to finish the preparations for the graduation ceremony. Besides, Lady Brentfield was most emphatic about the type of teacher she wanted: quiet, unassuming, dutiful. I was certain you fit that description."

Nearly every teacher at the Barnsley School fit that description, but Hannah could see by the steel in Miss Martingale's eyes that further argument was useless. She considered for a moment tendering her resignation right that moment, but she needed her final two weeks of salary and all of her commission money if she was to have enough to live in London.

She had been planning the move for years, traveling to the metropolis to become a portrait painter. For so long it had seemed outside her grasp. She had no formal training, after all. But just three months ago, the Earl of Prestwick had inquired whether the school's art teacher would be willing to attempt a portrait of the dowager countess. It was well known about Barnsley and the surrounding villages that Lady Prestwick was a gentle, retiring soul, easily frightened by the world around her. She was seldom seen outside the gates of her fine estate.

Hannah had been more than willing to paint the

beautiful countess, who put her in mind of Elaine in the legends of King Arthur. Elaine had pined away for her love of Lancelot, and it seemed to Hannah Lady Prestwick's sad smiles mirrored a similar melancholy. The resulting painting had been heralded by the earl and the local gentry alike as a fine work of art.

Since then, Squire Pentercast's lovely wife had requested that Hannah undertake a painting of their family. In addition, one of the more influential of the parents, the Duke of Emerson, whose daughter Lady Emily was one of Hannah's favorite and most promising students, had suggested that she paint him on his return from Vienna. As the squire's wife was well known in social circles, and the duke was a famous diplomat, Hannah was assured of at least the beginnings of a promising career. It was more than she had ever hoped for.

She had planned to finish her painting of the Pentercasts by Easter and put in her notice to Miss Martingale shortly thereafter. With the money from her two commissions and what she had saved working at the school for the last three years, she would have enough to live frugally in London for a year, building her reputation and her clientele. For the first time in her life, her dreams were within her grasp.

All she had to do was survive this trip to Brentfield.

"I tell you it will be a week to end all weeks," Priscilla Tate declared now as they settled into the carriage her aunt had sent for them, a shiny black with silver accouterments. The silver and black emblem on the side had told Hannah that those must be the Brentfield colors. She had tried not to be concerned that the emblem on the Brentfield crest was a wild cat rending a stag in twain.

Now Priscilla positively preened as the coach set off from the school. With the girl's golden blonde hair and emerald eyes, she was by far the loveliest of the graduating class. She was also one of the least popular, for all her considerable family connections. Priscilla had a way of lording her beauty and accomplishments over her classmates. Hannah had long ago begun to think of her as Hera Among the Lesser Goddesses.

"Your aunt is beyond generous!" This from Daphne Courdebas, the most athletic of the graduates. Everything about Daphne was long and lean, from her limbs to her light brown hair. And all of it had a tendency to tangle unmercifully in her unbridled enthusiasm for life. Amazon in Training, Hannah thought.

"And her still in mourning! How kind!" Ariadne Courdebas put in. At a year younger than her sister, Ariadne could easily have been from another family entirely. She was round and baby-faced, with lank brown hair, great vapid blue eyes, and a mind that latched onto every inch of printed material it could find, from plays to poetry and all types of facts. Recently it had been medical treatises, which had sent the girl to the nurse a dozen times over the last month over some imagined disease. It was amazing how truly distress could be mirrored on that round face, like Lot's Wife on Looking Back at Sodom.

"She's no doubt destitute in sorrow from the loss of her husband and stepson," put in Lady Emily Southwell. The Priestess of Delphi, Hannah thought, her artist's mind painting the picture. Lady Emily would have made such a marvelous seer. Her deep-set brown eyes, black frizzy hair, sallow complexion, and pinched nose were perfectly matched to her dismal view of the world. She even wore the dark colors and austere tailoring, like the brown silk gown that was nearly as depressing as Hannah's stiff black bombazine uniform.

Nonetheless, Lady Emily was the only one of Hannah's students who had shown the least promise as an artist at the Barnsley School for Young Ladies. Hannah was sure that it was her own recognition of Lady Emily's promise, as well as Hannah's talent, that had resulted in

Lady Emily's father, the Duke of Emerson, suggesting that Hannah paint him as well.

"Spending time with the new earl will prove compensation," Priscilla predicted with an arched look.

Lady Emily leaned closer. "Even after their mysterious deaths? I heard the rumors."

Surely this was unseemly conversation for four young ladies. "Girls," Hannah started.

They ignored her.

"Rumors?" Ariadne asked, sitting up straighter where she was squished between her sister and Lady Emily. "What sorts of rumors?"

Lady Emily's look darkened. "The previous earl and his heir were killed in a coaching accident eight months ago. I heard Farmer Hale telling Cook when he brought the milk that he heard from one of the tenants of the estate that it was no accident. When the grooms investigated, they found the carriage had been tampered with. Charles Tenant, Earl of Brentfield, and his son Nathan, Viscount Hawkins, were murdered."

"Girls," Hannah said more forcefully, a tingle running through her.

Ariadne gasped. "Were there no investigations? Did no one come forward with evidence?"

Priscilla tossed her curls. "There was no need for evidence. It's all a Banbury tale, I promise you. Lord Brentfield and his son were well liked, and there was no one in line to inherit. There wasn't even another heir in England. When the solicitors traced the family lineage, the fellow they found to inherit was so far removed that he couldn't possibly have planned a murder. He's a Yank, of all things."

The other three girls looked so suitably amazed by this fact that Hannah was able to turn their conversation onto another tact.

But as the short journey wore on, the girls grew more restive.

"We shall all be crushed inside this carriage," Lady Emily promised after they had bumped some distance from Barnsley. "He'll roll it on the next curve, you wait and see."

"Lord Brentfield's coachman seems quite competent," Hannah assured her, only to bite her lip as the carriage hit another rut.

"I think I shall be sick," moaned Ariadne Courdebas beside Lady Emily. Her gloved hands hovered in front of her trembling lips, and Hannah felt her own stomach lurch just looking at the girl's pale face. To her relief and the girl's embarrassment, all that erupted was a ladylike hiccup. Ariadne's face turned a healthy pink that matched her pink pelisse.

"I think you're simply excited," Daphne exclaimed on the other side of her, bouncing so vigorously with each bump that she set the blue silk ribbons on her pelisse fluttering. She enthusiastically poked her sister in her well-padded ribs, sending Ariadne into Lady Emily and Lady Emily into the equally well-padded wall of the coach. Lady Emily glared, and Ariadne clutched her side as if she'd been kicked by a horse. Hannah sighed and uttered a prayer for patience.

"Well, you should be excited," Priscilla said with a sniff, where she sat beside Hannah. "If it hadn't been for the countess's invitation, you'd all be cooling your heels at the school during Easter holiday."

All three girls colored at the reminder.

"It was very kind of her ladyship to invite all of us," Hannah told Priscilla, determined to put on a pleasant face. "I'm sure a week at Brentfield will be most educational."

Emily grunted, Ariadne grimaced, and Daphne nodded in agreement. Priscilla eyed Hannah thoughtfully.

"You say educational as if we were the ones to be educated, Miss Alexander," she replied, smoothing down the skirts of her lavender wool traveling dress. "You might find you'll learn something as well. I don't suppose you ever went out much in Society before you became a spinster."

It took all of Hannah's strength not to return the unkind remark with one of her own. She was aware that she was on the shelf, but somehow the reminder rankled. Her own mother, widowed at a young age, had tried to raise Hannah and her younger brother Steffen as their knighted father would have wished, but it was clear from the outset that Steffen must receive the schooling and training to make his way in the world. Hannah, it was hoped, would marry a country squire and raise children. But Hannah had fallen in love, with her painting.

Given the choice of marrying an elderly vicar like her grandfather or finding a post, she had elected to apply for the position of mistress of art at a school in faraway Somerset. Hannah was probably the most surprised of anyone when she had been given the job.

"I'm sure we'll all learn something," she replied to Priscilla, hoping her slight frown would reinforce her meaning that Priscilla had things to learn as well, such as manners. As usual, the subtle look was lost on the girl.

"I don't see how," Ariadne muttered. "Priscilla's already admitted that there won't be any young men."

Hannah shook her head at their obsession. "Come now, Ariadne. There is more to life than flirtations."

At that, they all protested, forcing her to hold up her hands in mock surrender.

"But Miss Alexander, how are we to practice for the Season?" Ariadne cried. "We have only a few weeks left before we are presented, and Miss Martingale has yet to allow us a single male on whom to practice our wiles."

"And I'm sick of playing the boy every time we practice waltzing," Daphne put in.

"And I of playing the boy while everyone tries their insipid conversations," Lady Emily grumbled.

Priscilla made a face, somehow managing to look charming at the same time. "There you go complaining again. Isn't a week in the country better than staying alone at school?"

"Easy for you to say," Lady Emily muttered. "You have a beau waiting for you at Brentfield."

Ariadne clapped her hands over her mouth as if she'd been the one to spill the secret.

"You weren't supposed to tell!" Daphne scolded.

Hannah glanced around at the three worried faces and Priscilla, who preened once again. She had a sudden vision of a strapping farmer's son riding up on a stallion and sweeping the fair Priscilla off to Gretna Green the moment the coach stopped at Brentfield: Hades Carrying Off Persephone. The elopement would surely be followed by the outraged Lady Brentfield demanding Hannah's resignation. Worse, her reputation would be ruined—she might never get another commission.

"Beau?" she ventured, almost afraid to hear the answer.

Priscilla's eyes glowed. "My aunt the countess is arranging for me to marry the new earl."

Hannah gaped. "But he's your cousin, and he must be years older than you are."

"He isn't my cousin," Priscilla maintained. "He is a distant cousin of the previous earl, who was my aunt's second husband. My father is related to her first husband. And he isn't so terribly old. He's younger than Mother."

Hannah opened her mouth to comment, then thought better of it. She could not imagine why a man would want to marry a near-child he hadn't even met. It was certainly natural, she supposed, that he felt some duty toward the widowed Lady Brentfield, but he hardly had to marry her niece.

The description of the chaperone Lady Brentfield had requested suddenly struck Hannah anew. Her ladyship had wanted someone quiet, unassuming, dutiful. Priscilla's confession proved what Lady Brentfield was seeking: someone who would keep the other girls occupied and provide no competition to the beauteous Priscilla, either in looks or in trying to ingratiate herself with the new earl. Hannah, more interested in her art than Society, was a perfect choice. She wondered whether Miss Martingale had known, or whether Hannah had truly been the only teacher available.

"You see, Miss Alexander," Ariadne grumbled. "It's just as I said. She'll spend all her time billing and cooing, and the rest of us will be bored to flinders."

"Lady Brentfield is far too good a hostess, I'm sure, to invite you to no good purpose," Hannah replied, hoping she was right. "She must have all sorts of diversions planned for your visit."

Lady Emily looked unconvinced, but Ariadne and Daphne brightened. As graceful as a bird, Priscilla waved a languid hand at the passing scenery.

"You will find out soon enough," she told them. "We are about to enter the estate."

Daphne and Ariadne scrambled over Lady Emily for a view out the carriage window. Only Priscilla sat back in her seat, arms crossed under her breasts. Hannah, however, could not resist a look out her own side of the carriage.

Since leaving the school shortly after Palm Sunday services, they had circled the west end of the Mendip Hills, passing by the village of Wenwood and running over the River Wen. Shortly thereafter, they had passed through vineyards, vines greening with spring. Now a two-story stone gatehouse came into view. The carriage slowed. An elderly man clambered out of the house and set about opening huge wrought-iron gates topped by balls of gold. As the gates swung open against stone columns, the horses sprang through. The man offered the girls a deep bow.

Hannah knew she should sit back in her seat and not gawk like her charges, but she had never seen such grandeur. Majestic oaks crowded on their left, and an emerald meadow dotted with jonquils swept away on the right. The meadow led up to the placid waters of a reflecting pond, which mirrored the front of a rose brick great house. The drive led up over a white stone bridge arching the stream that fed the pond and onto a circular patch of white gravel encircled by a shorter wrought-iron fence with gold balls on each post. A gate from the drive opened to a garden-edged path that led up to the porticoed porch of Brentfield.

Hannah stared. The wings of the house led off in each direction, three floors full of huge, multipaned windows edged in white. Liveried footmen as smartly dressed as the house strode out to assist the girls in alighting. Grooms sprang forward to hold the horses. The girls crowded past her, giggling and chattering. Hannah was so mesmerized that she didn't even realize they had all left until a footman peered into the coach and started at the sight of her.

"Can I help you down, miss?" he asked. Hannah blinked, then offered him her hand. Her half boots crunched against the snow-white gravel. She gazed upward, holding her straw bonnet to her head with one gloved hand, staring at the three golden urns that topped the pedimented porch.

"They tell me," said a warm male voice, "that the house was designed to mimic Kensington Palace."

"I was thinking of Olympus, actually," Hannah replied. She glanced at what she had thought was another footman and froze. Standing beside her was a gentleman who took her breath away. A Modern David in the Field, her artist's mind supplied, noting the tweed trousers and jacket. She wondered whether she'd brought enough brown with her to capture the warmth of his thick, straight hair. She'd need red for highlights too, or perhaps gold. No, she'd paint his eyes first, a deep, soft blue that would change, she would wager, with what he wore. And she would have to find a way to immortalize that welcoming smile, tilting more at one corner as if her wide-eyed stare amused him.

And she was staring, she realized, although she couldn't seem to help herself. She wanted to commit every detail to memory, as she did before painting a subject. She wanted to remember that his lower lip was more full than his upper lip, and both were a seashell pink. There were a dozen other things she needed to catch if she was to capture the man on canvas.

"Are you all right?" he asked when she remained silent in study.

He spoke with an accent, a twang that softened his speech. She had heard French, German, and Gaelic at the school, but she did not think this accent was a result of their influence.

"Yes, I'm fine," she managed. She glanced about and found that the footmen were tossing down the luggage from the top of the carriage and the boot. The man beside her appeared invisible to the servants, who bustled past with loaded arms.

He was equally invisible to the groomsmen who held the horses. None of them met his gaze as he glanced about. She wondered suddenly whether her bemused brain had conjured him, like a fairy from a mushroom circle, to grant her wish to paint. But no fairy she had ever read about dressed like a shepherd.

"You're the chaperone from the Barnsley School?" he asked politely.

He was making conversation, and she was gawking

again. She forced a smile. "Yes. I'm the school's art teacher."

A light sprang to his eyes, making her catch her breath anew. "You're an artist? What medium?"

"Oil painting," she replied a little surprised at his interest. "Although I like charcoal as well. There is a way of shadowing that gives the subject depth." Realizing she sounded as if she were lecturing, she blushed.

"Do you prefer landscapes, objects, or people?" he prompted eagerly.

"People," she answered.

"Classical or portrait?" he quizzed.

She was beginning to feel like the student for once. "Classical," she responded before she could think better of it. Then, knowing how scandalous that confession was, she quickly corrected herself. "That is, I hope to one day paint portraits."

"Have you studied, then?" he asked. "Would you know a classical piece if you saw one?"

Was this some kind of interview? She seemed to remember being asked such questions when she had arrived at the Barnsley School.

"I am self-taught," she told him proudly. "My family did not have the funds to send me to school. But I can assure you I know the Masters."

He grinned. "Then maybe I could show you a few of the Brentfield pieces."

She looked at him askance, still trying to determine why he was so interested. She had met few who were interested in her painting, even among those she painted. "Are you an artist, too?"

His smile deepened. "I've been called that a few times. But I work in leather, not paper or canvas." He held out his hands, which she saw were stained brown. His smile faded. "Although my badge of honor looks like it's wearing off. The mark of a gentleman, I guess."

Even with his gentle voice and accent, he made it sound as if being marked as a gentleman was a shameful thing. He shook himself and offered her a smile that was a pale copy of his original. "I'd love to see your work. And I do have a project that I'd like your help on. You'll be staying until Easter, I hope?"

"As long as the girls need me," Hannah replied. Belatedly, she glanced up the drive after her charges. Not a single girl was in sight. She rolled her eyes at her own ineptitude. Her first assignment as a chaperone, and she hadn't even escorted them into the house!

A tall, elderly, dark-skinned gentleman in tan knee breeches, navy coat, and the undisguisable air of command, was making his way toward them. Othello Coming to His People, her bemused brain suggested.

"I'm in trouble now," her companion murmured. "Derelict in duty once again." He heaved a sigh, but the twinkle in his eye told her he was hardly sorry.

"You're needed inside," the older man intoned with a nod. Hannah wondered why the Tenants would have use for their own in-house leather craftsman, but she felt a shiver of pleasure that she would be able to see him again during her visit. Perhaps she might find a moment to help him with his work here.

The older man turned to her with a bow. "You'd be the Miss Alexander for whom the young ladies are searching?"

"She's still beside the carriage, so they can't be searching very hard," her David quipped. "Now, don't glare, Asheram. You wouldn't want to reduce me to a quivering pulp in front of Miss Alexander, would you?"

"Perish the thought," the man replied.

"Good. Earn your keep and introduce me the way you tell me these Brits insist on."

The older gentleman rolled his wide-set eyes. "If you

would be so kind as to tell me your first name, Miss Alexander?"

Her David leaned forward as eagerly as when he had asked about her painting and set her blushing again. "Hannah," she murmured.

"Miss Hannah Alexander," the man said solemnly. "May I present David Tenant, Earl of Brentfield?"

Learn more at
www.reginascott.com/ladyemilycapers.html

OTHER BOOKS BY REGINA SCOTT

Fortune's Brides Series
Never Doubt a Duke
Never Borrow a Baronet
Never Envy an Earl
Never Vie for a Viscount
Never Kneel to a Knight
Never Marry a Marquess
Always Kiss at Christmas
Never Pursue a Prince
Never Court a Count
Never Romance a Rogue
Never Love a Lord
Never Beguile a Bodyguard
Never Admire an Adventurer

Grace-by-the-Sea Series
The Matchmaker's Rogue
The Heiress's Convenient Husband
The Artist's Healer
The Governess's Earl
The Lady's Second-Chance Suitor
The Siren's Captain

Uncommon Courtships Series
The Unflappable Miss Fairchild
The Incomparable Miss Compton
The Irredeemable Miss Renfield
The Unwilling Miss Watkin
An Uncommon Christmas

Lady Emily Capers
Secrets and Sensibilities
Art and Artifice
Ballrooms and Blackmail
Eloquence and Espionage
Love and Larceny

Marvelous Munroes Series
My True Love Gave to Me
The Rogue Next Door
The Marquis' Kiss
A Match for Mother

Spy Matchmaker Series
The Husband Mission
The June Bride Conspiracy
The Heiress Objective

The Regent's Devices Trilogy
(writing as R.E. Scott with Shelley Adina)
The Emperor's Aeronaut
The Prince's Pilot
The Lady's Triumph
The Aeronaut's Heart

Frontier Matches
The Perfect Mail-Order Bride
Her Frontier Sweethearts
Frontier Cinderella

And other books from
Harper Collins, Mirror Press, and Revell.

ABOUT THE AUTHOR

REGINA SCOTT STARTED writing novels in the third grade. Thankfully for literature as we know it, she didn't sell her first novel until she learned a bit more about writing. Since her first book was published, her stories have traveled the globe, with translations in many languages, including Dutch, German, Italian, and Portuguese. She now has more than 65 published works of warm, witty romance, and more than one million copies of her books are in reader hands.

Alas, she cannot have a cat of her own, as her husband is allergic to them. Fortune the cat belongs to her critique partner and dear friend Kristy J. Manhattan, who supports pet rescue groups and spoils her four-footed family members. If Fortune resembles any cat you know, credit Kristy.

Regina Scott and her husband of 35 years reside in the Puget Sound area of Washington State. She has dressed as a Regency dandy, driven four-in-hand, learned to fence, and sailed on a tall ship, all in the name of research, of course. Learn more about her at her website at www.reginascott.com, where you can sign up for her newsletter and receive exclusive free stories to read, including one from the Fortune's Brides series.

www.ingramcontent.com/pod-product-compliance
Lightning Source LLC
Chambersburg PA
CBHW070502300726
48975CB00007B/2282